Fallen Between

The Fallen Favorites, Volume 1.5

Amelia Rose

Published by Amelia Rose, 2025.

• • • •

ISBN: 9798990211759 (eBook, wide Distribution)
ISBN: 9798990211766 (Paperback, wide distribution)

• • • •

Written by Amelia Rose
Cover Design & Chapter Illustrations by Amelia Rose
Book typeset by Draft 2 Digital

DEDICATION

Special credit for this book goes to my older sister, Natalie, and the band Voilà.

While a few suggested that I write *something* about the time between books 1 & 2, it wasn't until my sister said something in passing, in our hotel room after an amazing Voilà concert, that something unlocked in my brain.

The next day I started writing what was supposed to be *at most* a novella. Five weeks later, I typed "the end" on a *slightly* shorter book than my norm.

So this is for you, Natalie. This wouldn't exist if you hadn't watered the seed at the exact right moment.

And if anyone wants to listen to a good theme song while you read this, try:

But What if I Fly, by Chrissy Costanza.

A Brief Content Warning

Hello reader, this book is a little milder than book 1, but there are still a few things to mention that may be considered triggering for some readers. The short list includes: Mild violence, depictions of panic attacks, references to suicidal ideation, drug use, psychological manipulation, open-door sex scenes, and first-person account of drowning. Your mental state and health are important, so please take care of yourself first. Yes, there are open-door sex scenes (2 of them), but feel free to carefully skip past them.

• • • •

But if you have made it this far and aren't perturbed, then you will enjoy this small addition to my vampire thriller series!

AUGUST

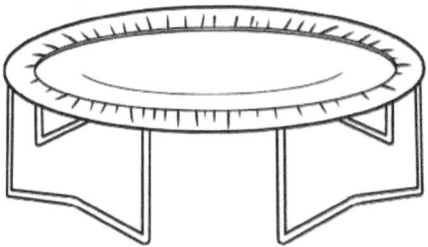

CHAPTER 1

DANIELLE

"I 'll curl up in the middle, and you jump as hard as you can to bounce me into the air!" Caoimhe said between giggles. Her dark braid wagged behind her to the rhythm of our bounces.

"Where I'm from, we call that 'Popcorn,'" I told her by way of agreeing.

I slowed to a stop on the trampoline. It took several seconds for the spring-taut surface beneath us to stabilize, but once it did, Caoimhe curled her small body into a tight ball in the very center.

"Ready?" I asked, preparing my knees to launch myself into the air again.

Her loud anticipatory laugh was my signal to jump. I tried to come back down onto the trampoline surface with more weight than my thin frame possessed to launch her into the air. Her curled form lifted off the surface, and she uncurled while midair, like the fluffy interior popping out of a kernel. She released a shrill cackle as she bounced and rolled out of it onto her back, her arms flopped to the sides.

I dropped carefully to my knees and rolled onto my back next to her, breathing heavy thanks to the exertion of the past several minutes. Though I was panting, something close to laughter was tickling my chest, and I hadn't felt that in months.

"I think that's it for me for now," I told Caoimhe, still struggling for a full breath. I sat up and crawled to the edge of the trampoline. "That's more movement than I've done in...a long time."

I missed the sun, and I missed exercise. I'd always been in great shape, thanks to track in high school and running consistently even after high school. But that was before I'd been dragged through hell.

"You should get out more," Caoimhe said, as if reading my thoughts.

"Yeah, well, your parents don't like me doing that." I tried to keep the bitter annoyance out of my voice. I climbed down and shoved my feet back into my slippers.

"Yeah, well, they can't stop you if they aren't here, can they?" she said, mimicking my American accent, which was jarring to hear because her Irish accent was usually so overpowering it was hard to understand her.

She loved mimicking me, and she loved teasing me for my American ignorance. I thought she'd never stop laughing when she saw me enter her name into my phone—spelling her name "Keeva" like it sounded when she spoke it—and her laughter had a second wind when she saw my baffled face as she typed the correct spelling into my phone.

I enjoyed her laughter, though, even if it was often at my expense. The nearly thirteen-year-old had volatile mood swings, which I understood from my memories of being her age. But I preferred her jovial moods and teasing laughter to attitude. I'd had enough *attitude* aimed at me from all sides over the past few months, so the reprieve was nice.

"True, they're not here, but I told them I'd keep an eye on you," I reminded her, kicking her shoes toward her as she hopped down from the trampoline.

"I don't need looking after," she said with a grimace, sticking her fists on her hips. "Go on and go. I won't narc. Go for a run. Go make a friend your age. Do whatever. Just, if you do, bring me back some sweets from the tuck shop."

Even if the rest of it sounded exhausting, the last part was almost enough to tempt me. Caoimhe had introduced me to Irish pick-a-mix sweets, and I was hooked.

"Maybe another time. I'm honestly good today. And the furthest thing from stir-crazy." It was mostly the truth.

I was better today than I'd been in a while. I hadn't taken the sleeping pills in two nights, which usually kept me in a fog even during the day. And it helped that the sun was shining for the first time since I'd arrived in Bray. Even though it was below sixty degrees in late August, the rare sunlight and the long, lush grass made the sleepy coastal atmosphere feel homey. If I closed my eyes and ignored the salty breeze, I could pretend I was back home in Colorado, beneath the mountains.

Caoimhe breathed a deep sigh and stomped away dramatically. She stopped at the firepit, a few feet from the Flynns' patio, and shifted on her feet, as if she couldn't stand still. I followed her and sat on the brick enclosure. Despite it being only sixty degrees out, the trampoline had warmed me enough that I was almost sweating. I peeled off my hoodie and tossed it aside, revealing a Lonely Vagrants shirt I'd stolen from Riley.

"If you won't go anywhere, then...can you show me?" she asked, averting her eyes from the pink scars marring my bare arms and instead looking into the firepit.

"Show you what?" I asked, though I already guessed what she wanted.

"Exactly what *my parents* don't want you to," she said, smirking. She stalked away but was back almost immediately. She tossed a large, dry branch into the firepit, then crossed her arms and frowned at me. "Go on. Light it."

"Caoimhe, that's not a good idea..." I mumbled weakly. I curled my hands into the folds of my T-shirt and realized for the first time how roomy the shirt was now. Riley wore his clothes baggy. But baggy on his rail-thin frame used to mean his shirts fit me as they should.

"Exactly why we should do it!" She waved her arms dramatically and pointed both hands at the wood in the firepit. "Come on! Screw their uptight rules. You need to let off some frustration! Light it!"

Playing with the leather bracelet around my right wrist, I wanted to argue that her parents weren't just uptight. But I held my tongue. She wouldn't get it.

Despite my wanting to reproach her, I couldn't keep the amused smile off my face. Her fiery, rebellious attitude could be contagious.

"They'll be able to smell the smoke," I argued, despite the pull to disobey.

"No, they won't." She waved her hand dismissively. "I'll spell the scent of firewood away. *That's* easy."

I wouldn't know, I kept myself from saying. I would've loved to know a simple, easy spell of *any* kind, but the Flynns kept me in the dark.

The last fragment of my resolve snapped, and I stood and faced the firepit. I pulled the stupid dampening bracelet off my wrist and tossed it onto my discarded hoodie.

The bracelet was meant to block the wearer from performing magic, and I was strongly encouraged to wear it at all times—especially when sleeping.

My time with the Flynns had started out okay, but it was far from the family reunion I'd half expected. They'd agreed to take me in and teach me, but they did it mostly out of curiosity and because they wanted to prove I was lying about my anomalous power.

While they weren't unkind outright, they could be condescending at times. I didn't press them too hard about teaching me anything, as I was still reeling from trauma and drowning in grief. I figured they'd teach me once I settled in.

We'd grown impatient with each other after mere days, though. I couldn't sleep, and when I did, I had nightmares that woke the house with my screams. They grew snippy with me because I kept them awake at night, and I grew snippy with them because I wanted sympathy and balance, but they provided neither. I pressed one final time for them to teach me something, and they lashed out with condescension—at last accusing me of lying just to have a roof over my head.

So I had shown them.

I picked up Caoimhe's wooden pencil and lit it. I didn't do it to scare them, but the fear came anyway. At first, I laughed their fear away, thinking they'd get over it and finally decide it was time to teach me.

Instead, out came the sleeping pills: heavy doses to keep me asleep all night and eliminate the risk of accessing my powers in my nightmares. Out came the bracelet for added security, day and night. I assured them that I'd never once unconsciously set anything on fire, but they didn't hear me. And, in truth, I didn't argue with them very hard.

I didn't really believe in the bracelet. I believed they underestimated my power. It wasn't pride: I'd just grown to accept that my anomalies always exceed expectations.

I welcomed the sleeping pills, though. Sure, they were eerily strong and kept me in a fog even during the day, but they let me sleep dreamlessly. And during the day, they numbed much of the pain of grief and the frustration that I'd left love behind for *this*.

The past two nights I'd fallen asleep reading before taking my meds and slept through the night without interruption. Now, fully lucid, I felt like *me* for the first time in weeks. Albeit, *me* didn't mean much when I was so bogged down with depression and grief, but egged on by Caoimhe's childish rebellion, my frustrated indignation of the past few weeks bubbled up to the surface. It wasn't much, but it could light a branch.

Caoimhe hopped beside me eagerly, but I ignored her and focused on the hunk of wood she'd chucked into the firepit. It'd be easy to light it, and it would be contained within the knee-high brick enclosure. What was the harm?

After a moment of concentrating on just the end of the branch, it sparked almost lazily, and a small flame appeared.

Caoimhe squealed but fell silent when I shot her a sharp glance. I raised my hand and twirled my fingers a little, imagining the flame curling down the branch like a snake. And, holy crap, it worked!

The flame coiled around the branch from nose to tip, just kissing the dry wood. It twitched eagerly, as if it knew I was denying it its food. I lowered my hand to my side, and the flame settled into the wood like a person relaxing into a hot bath. It resumed normal-flame behavior and devoured its hard-earned fuel.

Then the branch let out a loud crack and the flame burst outward. I jumped back in horror and glanced at Caoimhe. The wide smile she gave me was manic with sly joy, and she held up both of our hands between us. I hadn't noticed her grab my other hand. She was amplifying my power, even though I'd relinquished my control of the flame I'd made.

"Caoimhe, no," I said warily, returning my eyes to the flame. It grew even more, thanks to her influence, too big for the small amount of fuel the branch provided.

"Caoimhe, cut it out!" I told her as the flames grew higher. But she laughed jovially and jumped up and down beside me, her hand still clasping mine. "That's enough!"

The branch cracked, and sparks belched upward. I jumped back, but before I could pull Caoimhe with me away from the upblast, a pair of arms shoved me backward.

CHAPTER 2

DANIELLE

My hand ripped out of hers, in a fashion that instantly transported me back to that night in Rome when Alexis—

My back hit long, soft grass, not hard pavement. This sensation should have been enough to pull me back to the present, but it didn't. In one flash, I was in sunlit grass, with three forms above me—one was Caoimhe, I knew—and the next second I was in a dark alley with four figures circling.

"Fueco!" The word ripped from my throat, but I didn't mean to utter it. Back then, I'd foolishly shouted *fire* in my panic, because my parents had told me to in that type of situation. The irony of shouting it now didn't hit me immediately "Fueco! Fueco! Fu—"

"Yes, fire! Are you surprised, when you're the one that set it?" an irate female voice shouted down at me.

I could barely hear their shouting over the water rushing in my ears. I tried to scramble back, but I'd lost a slipper in the fall, and my socked foot slipped on the sleek grass. My shoulders collided with the ground again.

A hand slapped across my cheekbone—which did nothing to disrupt the panicked visions. I snarled, and my hands curled into claws to lash out at the figure kneeling over me.

The woman—Mrs. Flynn—reared back, and Mr. Flynn appeared in her place. He knelt and pinned my wrists to the ground with his hands.

"Easy, now," he said, but he sounded pissed instead of calm. "What the hell were you thinking?"

"I'm sorry!" I managed to choke out, blinded by tears. "I'm sorry!"

"Da, it was *me*! I made her do it!" Caoimhe shouted. "Can't you see she's freaked the feck out? Leave off!"

He pulled back, and I shot to my knees, ready to sprint away. But Mrs. Flynn grabbed my wrist and slapped the leather cuff bracelet firmly around it.

"This never leaves your arm again, do you hear me?" she said. Her mouth tightened into a hard line while she fastened it. "I liked you better when we thought you were just some band's discarded slut needing a place to stay."

I shot her a death glare.

"Yes, slut-shaming and *bondage*. Exactly the remedy for a violent fucking panic attack! You assholes!" The panic had faded, but not enough. And when I panicked, my tongue often grew bold. It always surprised me when the quips came out, but the shock on others' faces when my tongue grew a mind of its own was always satisfying.

"It's not bondage," Mr. Flynn sputtered, horrified by my crass humor. "It's to keep you safe. And keep all of us safe."

"And to keep me beneath you," I blurted before I could reel it back in. I hadn't had that thought before, but the inkling must have been stewing just beyond the drugged haze this whole time. I couldn't stop the words. "You wanted me to be a powerless *mutt* of a witch. And as soon as my magic proved otherwise, you sought to dampen it. To stamp it out."

"That's not it!" Mrs. Flynn held up her hands defensively, but her eyes still flashed with residual anger. "Your elemental power is rare. Rarer than rare."

"So rare that no one knows how to teach it," Mr. Flynn explained. "We're inept. But we don't want you to feel like you're not safe here. We just want us all to be safe. You don't have to be afraid of us—"

"I'm not fucking afraid of you," I said quietly. I knew my barely receding panic made it seem like I was afraid of *them*, but I'd faced far worse than a pair of middle-aged witches. "I know I'm safe, but it's not because of this." I shook my wrist in the air, indicating the leather cuff. "I'm not here because I'm afraid of my magic, or because things are after me. I'm here because I hoped for friendly faces that could help me heal from my fucking trauma. Instead, you just shoved sleeping pills at me and ignored me. But at least you sleep easy knowing I'm drugged and dampened."

The panic flared again in my chest. I could almost feel ice cold water rushing over my feet, filling an imaginary pool with no ladders.

"I'm more of a suicide risk than a fucking timebomb, you idiots," I said, desperate to be heard over the sound of the waves surging around my ankles that only I could hear. "I'm teetering over a chasm, and I need help, not restraint!"

"Danie—" Mrs. Flynn started, but I wasn't listening.

I lurched away from them and ran for the attic guest room that was my haven. The whole way there, I felt like I was wading through waist-high rapids, and they were chest high by the time I slammed the door shut with a crazed shriek.

I leaned back against the door and slid down to the floor, hugging my knees. I closed my eyes tight, braced my hands against the floor, and made myself count silently. At five, I pushed the air from my lungs. After another five, I forced myself to inhale, regardless of whether I inhaled water or air. If water, I'd die—kicking and thrashing—but that'd be that. If it was air, I'd still kick and thrash, but then I'd calm the fuck down on my own. I had to.

A scream welled in my chest as I inhaled, but I shoved my fist against my lips, so the air had no option of escape but through my nose. With that one breath out of the way, the rest came easier until I was confident I wouldn't scream. I wrapped my arms tightly around my legs and brought my forehead to my knees. The deep panic had passed, but it'd churned up all the heartache and despair in its wake, and now it sat heavy in my chest, raw and exposed, and it *hurt*.

What the fuck am I doing here? The thought kept circling as the ache forced a sob from my throat.

This place was no good. I'd hoped for welcoming arms, healing, and nurturing family. Instead, I got coldness, low-key condescension, and restraint. Felkyn had offered all the things I sought, but I'd pushed him away to figure things out on my own. Stupid. Stupid. Stupid.

I uncurled from the door and crawled to the small dresser that held my meager wardrobe and odds and ends. From the bottom drawer, I pulled out the cellphone the boys had given me. I sat on my bed and rested it on my lap while I waited for it to boot up and update.

As expected, there were dozens of notifications. Like an idiot, I'd signed into all of my accounts when I set up the phone. I should have anticipated the tidal wave of anxiety that came with logging back into social media accounts after being assumed dead for weeks, but I hadn't been thinking.

I'd been so solitary my whole life, with my family and Alexis's family as the only company I ever needed. After my abduction, I was sickeningly glad I'd been so unknown: it meant fewer people perished in the wave of the Kryrie's destruction.

But coming back from the dead gained me more attention than I ever wanted. And it was hauntingly jarring to see my own memorialized Facebook. Then, in coming back from the dead, the gushy, weepy posts weren't on my timeline anymore, they were in my DMs and my texts. I quickly ran out of energy to respond and buried the phone in my dresser, only pulling it out occasionally.

Of the dozens of notifications, none were from the one person I wanted to hear from. That wasn't surprising. I'd made him promise not to.

I needed him now, though. Fuck this place. Fuck my year-long healing journey. I needed him here now.

I pulled up his number, but my breath caught at the last second, and my finger froze above the green call button.

Just fucking call. He'll be here immediately.

But I stared at the screen, unable to breathe until the screen went dark. I let the air out of my lungs in a long, frustrated hiss. I unlocked the screen again and clicked on his contact image—a selfie he'd taken when he put his number into the phone—and enlarged it. I ran my fingers around the contour of his jawline, brushing them lightly over the curve of his smirking lips. They were the only lips I ever wanted to kiss, yet I couldn't push the call button.

As much as I wanted to see him, and as much as I wanted him to save me...I couldn't do it. I'd have to admit I'd made a colossal mistake in letting him go and needed him to save me.

But I didn't, did I? It was like I told the Flynns: no one was after me anymore, and I wasn't powerless. So what did I really need saving from? A panic attack I'd already pulled myself out of?

I powered the phone back off and hid it away again in the drawer. With a sigh, I sunk back onto the mattress and rubbed my hands over my face.

I could do this. The Flynns weren't *terrible.* They clearly disliked me, yet when I offered to compensate them for my stay—hell, Felkyn and Riley set me up with plenty of cash for incidentals—or to leave, they insisted it was fine and got almost defensive about it. They reminded me a little too much of Jeremy.

I'd had enough Jeremy energy for one lifetime, but this was different. I'd been in danger then, I'd been powerless and forced to stay with him. I wasn't stuck *here.* I wasn't staying out of necessity. I could easily leave.

I pulled my iPod from the bedside drawer and dug the headphones into my ears. I queued up my usual wallow music and, closing my eyes, curled up around a pillow.

I could save myself from this if it came to that. But not today. The lucid energy I'd found was spent, and the apathy of depression had leached into my bones post-panic attack.

FALLEN BETWEEN

Finding a way out of this mess was a problem for future Danielle.

SEPTEMBER

CHAPTER 3

DANIELLE

"Oy, did you hear me knocking?"

I flinched when the door of my room opened, but let out my breath when I realized it was just Caoimhe. I pulled my headphones out of my ears and looked at her sharply.

"Caoimhe, please don't just burst in here." I dropped my phone on the bedspread. "I'm jumpy, remember."

"Well, I was knocking." She demonstrated by rapping on the door in her signature pattern we'd agreed on and rolled her eyes. "When you didn't respond, I worried you offed yourself."

"Suicide jokes aren't cool, Caoimhe," I snapped tonelessly. I'd had a similar nihilist sense of humor at her age, but the jokes hit different after I'd attempted to kill myself back when I was at the end of my rope with the Kryrie.

"Sorry...woah!" Her face lit up when her eyes dropped to the bedspread in front of me, and she jumped forward into the room. "What's all that?"

I groaned inwardly, and my hands twitched toward the carefully arranged piles of makeup, as if to block them from her, but there was no point.

"Careful, please," I pleaded with her as she hopped onto the bed and bent her head down to inspect it all. "I don't want to make a mess, so don't open anything."

Showing a surprising amount of restraint given her excitement, she didn't reach for any of the product but instead ran her fingers lightly over an iridescent makeup brush shaped like a mermaid tail.

"These are gorgeous," she breathed, biting her lip as she picked up two brushes and twirled them in front of her.

"They were a gift," I told her, smiling sadly. "A very thoughtful and expensive gift, apparently."

I didn't know what possessed me to pull out the stash of makeup Felkyn had gifted me weeks ago. I'd spent the past hour inspecting all of it and googling the brands I didn't immediately recognize. I'd known he'd bought good, quality stuff, but just how much he'd spent on me was mind blowing. It was only a mild exaggeration to say that the pile of products and tools was worth its weight in gold.

"Speaking of gifts," Caoimhe said, pulling a box I hadn't realized she'd walked in with from behind her on the bed. "This arrived for you today."

"What do you mean 'arrived for me'?" I asked as she handed me the package. It was a cardboard box with my name scrawled on it.

"I mean, my parents opened the front door, and it was on the front porch, like an Amazon delivery, but...that." She waved her arm at the box.

Frowning, I opened the box, which wasn't even sealed with tape. Inside was a small stack of old books. By the titles on the spines, they all seemed to be either about witch history or the basic ins and outs of learning the craft. All the things the Flynns seemed against teaching me.

"I didn't know you were into makeup!" Caoimhe said, bringing my attention back to her. Once she saw that the contents of the box were just old books, she'd gone back to peering at the makeup laid out on the bed.

"I like keeping this air of mystery around me," I joked, swishing my hands in front of me, imitating smoke. I put the box on the floor by the nightstand and repositioned myself on the bed to face her. "I'm hoping to be a makeup artist. Eventually. It's kinda on hold at the moment..."

Back in June, I'd had an apprenticeship lined up for the fall in Fort Collins, Colorado. They'd reached out weeks after I resurfaced, and they still wanted me. I could go back, but the thought of returning to my hometown and all that waited there made me want to throw up.

"Were you going to put some on?" Caoimhe asked, carefully opening the lid of an eye shadow palette just enough to look at the colors inside. "These are cracker!"

"I don't know what I was going to do. I just wanted to look at them really." I shook my head, not knowing if *cracker* was good or bad. "I get more enjoyment out of doing others' makeup, though. Not so much my own."

"You could do me!" She placed the palette back in its pile and hopped onto her knees on the bed. She propped her chin on the backs of her fingers, mocking a model pose. "Please, please, please, do me! I'm a great canvas!"

It was tempting, but my gut-impulse was to sweep all the supplies back into their bag and hide them from ever seeing the light of day. They were expensive as hell and one of the most thoughtful gifts I'd ever received. Yet I didn't move.

What was the point of having the makeup if I was never going to use it? Felkyn wouldn't want me to hoard this stuff, so what was I waiting for?

But Caoimhe wasn't even thirteen yet, and I could imagine what her protective helicopter parents might say.

"I think your parents might actually kill me if I do that," I told her, grimacing. I held up a hand before she could argue. "And before you say we can do it sneakily, *no*. We can't. Because I don't have any makeup remover, and this stuff is tough to get off even with that. So until I get some of that, I can't use this stuff."

I remembered the trouble the boys had removing it after they'd convinced me to use their faces as canvases during one of those last days.

She pressed her mouth into a lopsided, pursed line and narrowed her eyes at me while she planned her next argument. I could see how she barely avoided rolling her eyes—progress.

"If that's all that's stopping you, I'll get us some." She stood up and walked to the door. "I bet me mam has some we can use."

"Keev, no—" I said, shortening her name phonetically in my haste. I reached out as if I could grab her, but she was too far. "Don't ask them. We can figure it out—"

She waved back at me without turning around, then she was gone. I let out a frustrated hiss and flopped backward on the bed. I didn't know exactly why I didn't want her parents to know even this much detail about me, but I felt they hadn't earned the right to know it.

It'd been a week since the firepit confrontation, and I'd kept almost completely to myself that whole time, only joining them for meals if I got stir-crazy enough. Otherwise, they brought me a plate and left it by the door, knocking to let me know it was there. Caoimhe talked to me at the dinner table when I joined them, but things were still icy between me and her parents.

It was hard to read them. They didn't ask anything about my past or the trauma I implied I needed help with. And they hadn't asked me anything about whether I was showering with the bracelet on—I wasn't—or if I was still taking the sleeping pills—I was only taking a quarter dose, if that. But they asked me if I needed anything when they made an Amazon haul the day after the incident and let me add items to the cart. So the helicoptering was less severe, but they still weren't interested in my overall well-being: just theirs.

I rolled carefully off the bed and connected the iPod to my new speaker and made sure my e-reader was charging—both items were my additions to the order they'd placed. I'd connected it to my new email and used Riley's payment information because I'd yet to sort out my own electronic finances.

I set my "Emo in 2009" playlist to a low volume and picked up the top book from the box I'd set aside. It seemed to be a basic starter book for witches. Cute. I lifted the cover and a folded piece of paper nearly fell out, but I caught it. It wasn't a note telling me who sent them, but just a triangle drawn in black ink.

When I heard footfalls on the stars, I set the book aside and braced myself for the Flynns' ire. But Caoimhe barreled through the door and jumped excitedly back to her seat on the bed. I raised my hands in time to catch the packet of makeup-removing wipes Caoimhe tossed at me.

"Let's do this!"

My mouth was gaping open stupidly in my surprise, and it took a few seconds before I managed to swallow any more "buts" in favor of doing the one thing that might bring me a little joy.

"I figured they'd want you to stay away from me," I told her once I sat down and asked her to pick a color for the overall look of her makeup.

"No, they've actually been like *annoyingly* pushy about encouraging me to check on you and hang out with you."

I nearly dropped the wipes in surprise and fumbled for a second before catching it. They'd encouraged her to check on me? They cared?

"But I kept telling them to cool it because you wanted space." She shrugged, handing me the shadow palette she'd chosen and pointing to a color.

"How did you...what clued you in?" I asked, surprised by her perception. Usually when she wasn't reading she was up in my business.

"You said everything was taken from you. Your...your family, right?" she asked with more care than I expected. I nodded but didn't say anything. "I mean...I lost my dog last year and it wrecked me—*wrecked me*—and that was, you know, a dog. But you lost...I just mean I can't even fathom that, but I figured you wanted to be left alone. Right?"

My hands tightened on the makeup palette I held as my chest tightened painfully. I bit my trembling lip, but I needed to sniff violently to keep my nose from becoming a faucet.

"Yeah, kind of. But not too much space," I said, my voice shaking a little. "They can treat me like a mental patient, but it doesn't mean you have to. I'll let you know when I get overwhelmed, okay? Deal?"

"Deal," she said, imitating my American accent, making me roll my eyes.

She was quiet while I planned a rough idea for her look based on the color she'd picked. I gave her a brief education in what each item was, but I didn't tell her what I planned to create with it.

"So...what did happen to you?" she asked carefully, after I started in on my art project. "You can tell me to shut it. But I'm a kid. I'm curious."

"You want the short version or the long, brutal, horrific story?" I asked with a smirk, squirting a thin line of tinted concealer to her cheek for contouring.

"Well, if you want a giving out from my parents, then the long, brutal one," she joked. From context, I could guess what "giving out" meant, and I didn't want another verbal lashing from her parents. "But I don't care. Tell me whatever you think my wee brain can handle."

I hesitated for a second to determine how much to share without giving her nightmares. "I was on vacation." I kept working on her face while I talked. "I was kidnapped by some very bad—people. And while they had me, they also went out and killed everyone in my life. Which is why I can't—and why I don't want to—return home just yet."

"Like serial killers?" she whispered.

"Worse," I said, but I wouldn't look in her eyes. "They weren't human, Caoimhe. And they hurt me. It's how I have all the scars on my arms, and this one." I pointed to the pink line through my left eyebrow.

"How did you get away? How are you not still afraid of them?"

"Well, you've heard my screams at night, Keev. Clearly, I'm still afraid of them on some level," I said with a small snort. "But I got out thanks to a group of men who saved me and sheltered me."

"The band? The Latent Vices or whatever?"

"Lonely Vagrants, yeah," I corrected her, dabbing her face with a makeup sponge. "They're Lapsi."

"A Lapsi rock band?" She snorted. "Like that one lame movie..."

"Mmmhmm," was all I said. "Incredibly long, sad story short, they sheltered me until we found a way to get rid of the bad guys for good. Then I came here. And even though I'm safe, and alive, I'm still a bit of a mess."

"And what's the slightly longer, juicier story?" she asked, smirking and waggling her eyebrows mischievously. "I feel like there's a lot more there, and what you said doesn't explain anything about how you got to be *here*, seeking my parents' help. And how you seem so...eerily confident yet ignorant."

I blew out a huff and rolled my eyes. She wasn't going to let me off that easily after all. I wanted someone to confide in, but I wanted to spare her young mind from the extent of the horror, at the very least. And while I trusted her, I didn't trust her not to unwittingly blab something to her parents.

"I'll tell you, but there are things I don't want your parents, or anyone, to know. It's for my privacy and my safety. Do you get it?"

She nodded, looking serious. She put a hand to her chest. "Definitely. It'll be in my sisterly confidence, I promise."

A sharp pain lanced through my heart when she referred to me as a sister, but at the same time the pain felt almost nice. I'd lost a sister already, and it was destroying me from the inside, but the idea of Caoimhe seeing me as a sister repaired one of the ragged edges of my wounded heart.

"All right, but if I ever feel like you're getting too close to sharing something I don't want you to, I'll give you a signal, okay?" I said once I recovered. I bit my lip, thinking what the signal could be. "Any time we want to communicate anything secretly, brush your eyebrow casually, like this, okay?" I demonstrated the signal, discreetly brushing my index and middle finger lightly over my split eyebrow.

"Got it," she said, mimicking the gesture but finishing with a wink. "Now spill."

With a deep breath, I dove deeper into the story. This time, I explained how I'd discovered over time that I had some anomalous witchy characteristics and abilities and covertly worked on honing them with Felkyn. I told her about the band being conscripted into helping a group of witches and about me becoming a bargaining chip in that deal, but I didn't name the group, and I didn't tell her anything about Jeremy's real identity and the group's failed plan at trapping and sacrificing him. I'd take that secret to my grave if I could help it.

"Why didn't you stay with the band, then?" she asked once I finished telling her as much as I dared. "Is it because you can't sing or play an instrument?"

"Heh, well, that's one reason," I said, grinning. "That and the fact that they aren't really a band anymore. It all fell apart, and the shirts I stole from them are about to be worth a lot of Euro."

"But you didn't like any of them enough to stay with one of them for a bit."

I narrowly avoided wincing and dropping the brush. "No, I liked them. And they liked me." I didn't feel the need to clarify that one of the bandmates had despised me, poisoned me, and tried to sell me. "And I liked one of them *very much*. But I need..."

"Space."

"Exactly."

We were quiet for a few moments while I finished her contouring and started in with multiple colors of eyeshadow on her temples.

"So do you use all these things every day?" she asked after a few minutes, motioning toward the products I wasn't using on this project.

"No, not normally. I haven't worn any makeup in months."

"Don't lie. Your eyes are *always* lined." She glanced at me sharply.

"Oh, it's not makeup, it's tattooed."

"No way!"

"Yeah." I ran a fingernail over my lash line and held it out to show nothing came off.

"You are the coolest person I know."

I smiled but didn't respond. I just continued with my design on her face.

"So, does the rest of the town know about me?" I asked after a few more minutes. Her temples and eyes were done, with just eyeliner and mascara to go. "I can only imagine what they've been telling everyone. That I'm a timebomb. More than they were prepared for. That I'm unstable."

"I don't know what they've been saying to other grown-ups. I tune all that out," she said with a shrug. At my instruction, she held still as a statue so I could line her eyes. "But I've been talking you up with all my friends. We're teens. We like unstable."

"So glad I have a good rep among the thirteen-year-olds..." I mumbled, still concentrating. Caoimhe's shoulders twitched while she held in a snort. "But I think I need someone my age, don't you?"

"You could find friends your own age," she gently teased. "If you ever left this house."

"*They* don't want me to, remember?" I grumbled, picking up the mascara and tearing at the plastic seal.

"You could sneak out. Haven't you ever snuck out of your home before?"

"No. Have *you*?" I looked at her with concerned horror.

"At twelve? No," she scoffed and rolled her eyes. "But, you know, it seems like something every teen does. Unless the tele lies?"

"The tele lies," I said, frowning.

"Well, even so. My folks aren't here all the time. And I could cover for you so you can sneak out. You can see the town. Buy more makeup remover. Get us candy."

"I don't know, Caoimhe. We'll see," I mumbled, opening the mascara. "Now, this is the last step and we're done. Hold still, open your eyes wide, and look *up*."

OCTOBER

CHAPTER 4

FELKYN

T he clasps of the violin case released with too much of a snap, which was a dead giveaway that the case and the instrument inside weren't quite as loved as mine. But few were, really, seeing as mine was an antique—a well-loved, well-cared-for antique.

It didn't matter how new this one was; I was borrowing it only for the moment. I stepped into the middle of the large studio, which was twice as big as the one I was used to. It felt *too* big, but once I put the bulky headphones over my ears and tucked the instrument under my chin, the whole world fell away.

The tune had been playing in my head for the past two months, starting with a few mournful notes the day I'd left Danielle in Ireland. It'd grown longer and taken shape every day since. But this was the first time hearing it on the violin, and it was perfect. The song needed a violin solo in the middle, before the bridge. I knew from my many dives into Danielle's mind that the violin was her favorite, so it fit.

With this, I had the whole melody, and I was nearly ready to sit down and attach lyrics to this song from my aching heart.

It'd been a long two months. Two months of dealing with the dissolution of a platinum and Grammy Award winning band. Two months of grieving a best friend as well as a niece. Two months of reeling from the betrayal of someone I'd trusted with my life—with Danielle's life. Two months with her song swirling in my head, demanding to be written.

When I wasn't writing, I filled up my time with surfing, either in Australia or at some of my favorite California beaches, pretending to be an amateur guitarist at open mic nights, or motorcycling around various cities.

I kept moving and kept busy. The nights were the worst. When once, I used to flirt and mingle for hours on end, dragging out the pleasurable feeding process for almost the entire night, now I couldn't hold anyone in my thrall for more than a moment before the guilt seeped in. Blood was an unfortunate necessity, and it was easy enough to remove the sexuality from the need, but as far as romantic companionship and chemistry—fleeting or not—I only wanted Danielle for that.

I'd start out each night looking for someone like her, but then I'd feel gross about it. I didn't want to feed on Danielle: I wanted to be *with* her. So instead, I'd seek out someone who wasn't like her to satisfy the thirst. But by then the mood was killed; once I started thinking about Danielle, I couldn't stop. I'd wonder whether she'd ever be found in such a venue. Was her hair longer by now, or was she keeping it short? Had she dyed the vibrant blue and purple streaks back to her natural brunette?

Within this circular thought pattern, I'd also realize I didn't know what she would've been wearing. I'd only seen her in borrowed lounge clothes and the few pieces she'd picked out on a hasty shopping trip with Jeremy. I had no idea whether she was a leggings girl, a sundress girl, or a skinny jeans, Converse, and T-shirt girl. I'd been in her mind so many times, yet I'd always steered away from any memories of her looking in a mirror, naked or otherwise.

So instead of enjoying my nightly outing, I ended up rushing through the usual motions of feeding so I could get home—wherever home was that week—and pore through her social media to try to satisfy my curiosity.

There wasn't much across her few accounts, though. Most of her photos were from her track and field days, formal high school dances, or snapshots of her working on actors' makeup during school shows. She hadn't posted anything new since before her abduction. Still, I kept going back: always thirsty for something tangible, even if it was just pictures.

I sure hoped she was faring better than I was, because I was bordering on obsession. I intended to respect the year timeline. And if she didn't want me at the end of it, I'd leave her alone forever. But what was I supposed to do with my feelings until the end of the year? Let the feelings burning within me die out—if they even could—or keep them at the same simmer until we see each other again? Like a good soup, I was fine simmering if that's what it took.

In the meantime, I needed to change my MO when it came to feeding: less nightlife, less flirting. Instead, I was working on a plan to rent a studio and start giving guitar or bass lessons. It would be easy to set up by using my contacts within the music industry to spread the word. I imagined my clientele would be the children of movie stars, famous musicians, and Hollywood execs. I didn't feed on kids or teens, but I could prey on their affluent parents without it tarnishing my conscience.

I reached the end of the melody and stood with the violin perched above my collarbone for another moment, savoring how the pose felt so natural after thousands of years. My first instrument had been the most basic of lyres, but I'd never felt complete until I tried a violin, in Italy sometime in the sixteenth century. Half a millennium later, my neck still naturally tilts to the left, and when I'm pensive, my jaw flexes, as if feeling for the chin rest of a violin.

Danielle had noticed this tick the first time we spoke. I'd challenged her to guess what I played, and if she'd had the chance to answer, she'd have been spot on. If that night had ended differently, I'd have been a lost man right then and there.

The lights in the studio clicked off as I snapped the clasps closed on the case. They flickered on again as I pulled off the big headphones and stood up, turning to the big picture window.

Riley stood on the other side of the glass, staring deadpan into the studio at me, his fingers flicking the light switch on and off every few seconds. When I turned his way, he lifted his eyebrows and jerked his head to the side in a quick "let's go" motion.

Despite the coldness in his expression, I couldn't help the smile that split my face at seeing my friend.

"Man, have I missed that closed-off, shy, deliciously innocent face of yours," I told him as I left the recording booth and closed the door behind me. "Yet the scowl is new. Come here!"

I didn't wait for him to be ready for me before I threw my arms around him in a bear hug.

I also hadn't seen him in two months, which helped me justify being so unhinged and inconsiderate. To go from living with three friends and finding love to being completely alone once again left me in more of a spiral than previous times when the forced loneliness reared its ugly head.

"Jesus, it's like hugging a broom," I mumbled loudly while still hugging him. He was thin as a beanpole and remained completely rigid in my embrace. "Come on, man, for me?"

He released a huff and his arms went stiffly behind me and patted my shoulder blades once. The begrudging affection made a laugh bubble up in my throat, which I held at bay as I released him.

"It's good to see you, man," I told him, dropping the playful tone. "I know you want space, but I want you to know I'm available. The curse isn't loud right now."

"Maybe not for you," he mumbled, his shoulders giving a quick jerk upward in the most apathetic shrug I'd ever seen. "But it's all still...much."

"Thanks for coming to this anyway. I wish it was a happier thing we're doing. Like accepting an award or something."

"I don't even get why you need me." He shook his head and ran a hand through the back of his hair.

"Because this is our baby, Riley," I told him, my eyebrows drawing together. His face twitched at the word *baby*, probably thinking I was about to call him by the pet name I usually used for him. "And I know it sucks to have to say goodbye to it, but you *should* be here."

"It was your guys' baby. I was just dragged along for the ride."

I refused to believe that. While he was the youngest, he'd been in the music scene the longest of all of us. He could play any instrument by feel, and he'd toured with a number of musicians over the past several decades. For him to say this meant nothing to him was blasphemous. He was a shell of himself, and this blasé dismissal was just a front, but it still hurt to see him like this.

Before I could say anything in response, the outer door of the studio opened and Lorenzo's assistant poked her head in.

"Felkyn, Riley, now that you're both here, he's ready for you," she said, her cheeks coloring as she glanced between us.

This was nothing new. As Lapsi, we're almost embarrassingly pretty: frozen at our most attractive. Riley was practically gaunt but still devastatingly handsome. And me, while my blondness was fake—I dyed it millennia ago from its original mediterranean brown—my skin remained as golden as the day I was changed, and I had a complexion models would *kill* for.

CHAPTER 5

FELKYN

We followed the flustered assistant to the conference room where Lorenzo Vittorio, our manager, waited. He stood from his seat at the long, empty table and approached us. This man usually had a spring in his step no matter the occasion, his jovial Italian energy practically vibrating through his beer belly. But when he approached us today, everything was muted, bordering on somber. The bright green button-down he wore, unbuttoned to show a significant amount of chest hair on his burly chest, was the only indication of his usually colorful personality.

"Miei signori," he said, stopping in front of us. He gave me a brisk hug that I would have found weird for him, but my lonely, touch-starved ass leaned into it with a little too much enthusiasm. He released me and turned to Riley and, showing the restraint I lacked earlier, merely held out his hand, which Riley took, looking relieved. "No matter the why, it's so good to see you both. My prized darlings. Riley, I hope you know how sorry we all are. We tried to send flowers, but with you traveling, we didn't know where to send anything..."

"It's fine, really, flowers are...it's not necessary. But thanks," Riley mumbled, tripping over the words and no doubt chafing at the attention.

I pulled Lorenzo's attention back to me and laid on the charm, while keeping the tone sober and stoic. I guided us to the table where we took seats by the stack of paperwork. He mentioned that Jeremy had been there earlier to sign his portion of the legal documents and hinted his baffled frustration with the man.

Jeremy hadn't been there, though; it'd been me. With a healthy dose of mesmerism, I'd avoided all the security cameras and made everyone think it was Jeremy berating them and signing the dissolution documents. Masquerading as our long-haired, sour-faced ex-bandmate and further tarnishing his reputation had been entertaining, but it hadn't felt good to be so mean to Lorenzo, who I genuinely admired.

Which was why I lathered him with charm and sincerity now. After all, we were royally screwing him by breaking up the band. Colin's tragic death made it easier to justify cutting ties, but it still put Lorenzo in a rough spot and left him holding all of our collective bags.

As he distributed the paperwork we needed to sign, he gently prodded us for more information about the drama that destroyed the band prior to Colin's sudden death, but I sidestepped everything, using a minimal amount of mesmerism when needed. Colin had always been the idea guy, and without him, Riley and I were creative voids. So in the aftermath of the ordeal with the Agathati, we'd opted for an air of mystery around the band for fans to forever speculate on while we all retired from the limelight.

Finally, we got to signing all the legal documents, dissolving our contracts with our label and album artists, backing out of future collaborations we had on the books, and determining the future distribution of royalties—especially Colin's since he had no next of kin besides Riley.

The second stack of paperwork was the pile of NDAs *my* lawyers had sent to the label for Lorenzo and his associates to sign. They were magical gags, courtesy of the witchy lawyers we contracted when we started the band. In signing the documents, they physically couldn't spread any rumors about us or believe any that were spread by fans or insidious tabloids.

Lorenzo put his last remaining signatures on these forms and passed the stack to me, looking a little dazed as he did so—a side effect of the magical seals he'd unwittingly completed. Once they passed from his hands, the light returned to his eyes and he snapped back to business.

"There's one last thing I wanted to bring up. This is not so much a legal thing but a courtesy thing."

"Shoot," I said, tucking the forms into my bag.

"It's about the opening bands we were lining up for future tours." He folded his hands and rested them on the stack of documents in front of him. "Would it be okay if I shared their contact information with other bands? One American band in particular is planning an international tour and is poking around for openers to tour with them. I wanted to run it by you first before I started suggesting any."

My answer was an automatic yes, but I glanced at Riley to make sure he was in the conversation. He nodded once, his frown communicating that it was obviously fine with him.

"Yes, of course," I said eagerly. "You don't need to run something like that through the two of us. We scouted those bands and chose them because we believed in them. We'd never stand in the way of their success if we could help them."

I didn't understand why it was even a question. Then again, he hadn't asked "Jeremy" that question when I was there earlier.

Duh, I thought, almost rolling my eyes. Jeremy certainly would gatekeep out of spite. *Lorenzo, I knew I liked you, you smart man.*

"Good! Glad to hear it!" Lorenzo grinned, drumming his fingers on the table. "There's one band in particular I had in mind and was really hoping we'd be on the same page."

"What band?" Riley asked, leaning forward.

There we go, a small spark of the old Riley, I thought, keeping my face still so I didn't scare it off. Riley could *say* he hadn't cared about our journey as a band, but he couldn't hide his real interest for long. Especially when it came to touring and other bands. He'd *loved* touring.

"One of your favorites. Killer Craic," Lorenzo said.

Ah, yes. I remembered them. They were a small band with a vibe that matched ours. The lead guitarist was a new dad when we first met them and loved the idea of having his wife and small child visit him on points of the tour. The kid was probably three by now. And if I remembered correctly...

"They're based in Ireland, right?" I asked before I could stop myself. I sat up straighter in my chair and leaned forward

"Yes, a small town in Ireland, called—" He checked his notes, but I already knew. "Bray. But they're eager to travel."

"You think we should go see them one more time?" I suggested, biting my lip to keep from seeming overeager.

"No," Riley said firmly, unsurprisingly. Before I even started suggesting it, I'd felt him tense beside me.

"Just to fully vet them. Make sure they're good enough to pass along—"

"We already have. Twice," he argued flatly. "Lorenzo has things in hand. He doesn't need us on this anymore."

His piercing blue eyes flashed dangerously at me for the briefest second—too quick for Lorenzo to catch. I snapped my mouth shut and tried not to make my disappointment obvious.

Yes, I was foolishly imagining *accidentally* bumping into Danielle during such a visit to Bray. It wouldn't be breaking any rules if we were there on other business. But Riley was right to slap sense into me.

We wrapped up with Lorenzo and said our goodbyes with another bear hug for each of us—this one seemed to be less jarring for Riley. The goodbye was heartbreaking. I hated that Lorenzo got screwed as much as we did in the fallout. Thankfully, with the song I was working on, I might be able to work with him again one more time.

"Hey, Riley, I'm sorry for...suggesting we go to Ireland," I told him while we waited for the elevator. "You were right to shoot me down."

He nodded but didn't say anything. He pressed the call button again, as if it would get the elevator there faster.

"The truth is, I'm not coping as well as I thought I would. I miss her, and I'm dying for any kind of...details about how she's doing."

It was a poor choice of words, saying I was *dying* for something when Riley's brother had just died for Danielle. His mouth pinched, but I plowed on.

"Have you heard anything from her? *Anything*?"

"No, I haven't," he said shortly, pressing the button again. I knew he'd shift away from me if he could, but we'd been within sight of a security camera this whole time, so he wouldn't risk it.

"Nothing? At all? I mean, I was told to stay away, but not you—"

"It was implied that I stay away too, and I'm respecting it," he snapped, eyeing me sharply. "I'm leaving her alone to cope, like she wanted—like I wish people would leave *me* alone."

"I'm sorry for dragging you here," I told him again. "I wouldn't have if it wasn't legally necessary."

"*Please*," he scoffed. "We both know you forged Jeremy's signatures on these *legally necessary* documents."

Well, shit. I'm caught there. I pulled my hands from my pockets and held them up.

"You're right. Again. I dragged you out because I selfishly wanted to see a familiar friendly face. I told you, I'm not doing well..." I mumbled. I stared hard at him, hoping for a little sympathy to soften his sharp features. He let out a little huff, so I prodded back in. "Please, tell me anything. Anything if you have it."

"I really have nothing, man. Other than she's buying music again on our shared account and screwing my play counts all to hell."

"Really? What's she buying?" I asked, latching on. Her music taste might give some inkling into her state of mind. "Like, is she buying happy music or—"

"I think you're forgetting that she was never really a happy-music kind of girl. Aside from the musicals, she almost always listens to *angst*." He shrugged and ushered me impatiently into the elevator that had finally arrived. "I think she also has an e-reader now. She's using a new email, but *my* payment info for books. So she might be a shut-in still."

He meant it as a joke, but it flattened me to hear it. I knew she was grieving, but I didn't like imagining her as a shut-in. I hoped she was out experiencing life, honing her magic, or traveling even. Something in my disappointed face softened Riley, though.

"She started a new Instagram account," he said begrudgingly. "I shouldn't know about it, but when the mysterious e-book purchases started happening, I traced the email and stumbled onto the Instagram account she just opened."

"She did?" I asked, simultaneously placated by the news and exhilarated. It explained why she hadn't touched any of her other socials since resurfacing. New account, fresh start. The doors of the elevator opened into the lobby. "Any chance, I could..."

"I'll text it to you," he grumbled and walked past me out of the elevator. "Now, please, I love you, but fuck all the way off now."

"I love you, too, man," I called after him.

Without turning, he held up his middle finger as he walked out the door onto the street.

NOVEMBER

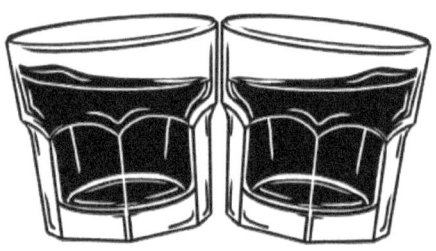

CHAPTER 6

DANIELLE

It was a feat sneaking out in the evening. I wasn't even sure if the sneaking out was necessary, but rather than risk the Flynns' disdain, I'd opted to embrace what Caoimhe misguidedly believed was a teenage rite of passage and snuck out of the house.

I was so flustered when I got to the bar that I barely noticed the patrons inside lean subtly away from me or the wariness on the bartender's face, which bordered on disdain. I just ordered the easiest thing—a rum and coke—and glued myself to the bar, clutching tightly to the crumpled flyer and its scribbled rendezvous note in a death-grip, while I waited for the sound of rushing water in my ears to quiet.

"Haaaaaaaal, whiskey, please. Make it a double!" a blonde girl called, startling me by stepping up to the bar directly beside me, despite the lack of crowd and the bartender at the other end of the counter.

I lifted my glass to my lips and edged aside a few inches to give her more room, but she leaned with me, her long blond waves brushing my shoulder as she glanced at me mischievously.

"No, no, no, hun," she chided me, putting her hand over the top of my glass and pushing it back down to the counter.

"Hal no doubt stiffed you on the alcohol because he's a scared piece of shit!"

She uttered the last sentence louder so Hal, who approached us with a bottle of amber liquid and a glass, could hear her reprimand.

I followed her gaze and this time clocked the disdain on his face, directed at me. It was the same look the cashiers gave me at the tuck shop when I visited. What little wind had returned to my sails in boldly embracing this little bit of freedom gusted away in one breath.

As my shoulders sagged, she draped an arm heavily across them and leaned her temple against mine.

"Thank you, Hal. We appreciate you looking out for our guest here, but she wants something more than just coke," the woman said. The smile disappeared from her face, and she stared hard at him. "My friend will have the same as me. On my tab."

"Aoife—" he started reproachfully, but her glare silenced him.

That's how you pronounce it, I thought, thankful he said her name aloud. I never would have guessed from the spelling that it was pronounced like "Ee-fa." Caoimhe had just laughed at my expense when I asked her.

Aoife stared him down for several seconds until he let out a huff and grabbed another glass.

While he filled each tumbler with ice and poured the two drinks, Aoife stepped away, and I took the moment to eye her, warily, to confirm it was the same girl from earlier. She was a few years older, a few inches taller, and enviably curvier than me, with skin as pale as mine, thanks to Ireland's gloom. She wore dark eye makeup around her gorgeous blue eyes and her long dark blond hair curled halfway down her back.

She turned to me. "I'm so glad you decided to come. I—" Her mouth fell slack as her gaze scanned around my eyes, and her lips curled from a surprised "o" into a giddy grin. "Oh my god, your makeup!" She breathed in awe. "Holy crap, you look stunning!"

A laugh bubbled up in my chest—a feeling so foreign, I almost choked on it. I opened my mouth to thank her for the compliment, but she gripped my chin firmly and turned my face this way and that, admiring my craftiness from every angle in the smoky lighting of the bar. My smile grew even more, despite the awkwardness of the face-grab, and my heart fluttered—a feeling somewhere between elation and heartache—at her attention.

I caught sight of myself in the mirror-backed bar shelves. My eyes were lined cleanly in black, heavier at the outer corners, and the mascara darkened and lengthened my lashes drastically. Both above and below my eyes, I'd blended eye shadow in all colors. The lazy curls in my hair hid the fact that it was growing out and looking less like a punk bob and more like the amateur hack job it really was. When unstyled—as it always was these days—it was past my collarbones and desperately needed attention. I'd been using my makeup on Caoimhe almost every day but rarely used it on myself. But since tonight was my first night out since my abduction in Rome, I'd gone all out.

"Seriously, it looks so professional. Do you do weddings? Or, like, fashion?" she gushed, releasing my face and leaning back on her heels.

"Um, no, I don't," I said, recovering my tongue. "I always wanted to. Not weddings, I mean, but other makeup work. I'm not doing anything now. I'm..." I stopped, not knowing how to say under house arrest tastefully.

"Locked in the attic except for a weekly trip to the tuck shop," she finished for me with a knowing smirk.

We'd collided outside the tuck shop where I was resupplying my and Caoimhe's stash of Irish sweets. Her band flyers, my precious iPod, and candy fell at our feet, but thankfully nothing was harmed or inedible. I'd walked away from the store with candy, wet knees, and a flyer for this event, with the words "Please come! Your friend, Aoife" scrawled in the corner. She hadn't scribbled the note after our collision, but before.

"It's a crime that they make you feel like a prisoner, but tonight you and I party and have a good time! Okay?" She lifted her glass, and I automatically did the same. We clinked glasses, and I took a careful sip of the straight whiskey. The burn hit my nostrils first, and thankfully I kept it from hitting the back of my throat. Still, I barely held down a cough. I opened my eyes and found her watching me, smiling like she couldn't believe I was here, when it should be me looking at her that way.

"Come on!" She grabbed my hand and pulled me away from the bar.

The bar was more crowded than a few minutes ago when I first ordered my drink. She practically skipped across the bar with her head high, and I kept my gaze on the floor between her and my feet, trying hard not to draw anyone's attention to me. But it was useless. I felt their eyes following us and boring into my skull. I was the town curiosity and the town freak. But it wasn't anger or judgment I felt skewering me: it was fear.

She brought us to a high-top table and set down her glass. As soon as I set mine down, she pulled me into a fierce hug. I froze for half a second but immediately melted into the embrace, burying my face in her shoulder. The last time I was comforted with something as simple as a hug was when I'd said goodbye to Felkyn. I'd been essentially isolated ever since.

"I'm just so happy you're here!" She practically squealed, pulling out of the hug and twirling me around, holding my hand aloft. I laughed and stumbled to a halt, already off balance from the swig of whiskey on an empty stomach. "I was so worried this wouldn't be your jam. But you're here, and the fact that you're wearing this—" She tugged on the hem of the front of my T-shirt, pulling the image on the front straight so she could get a better look at the cartoon hands making an L and a lude tongue waggling between the fingers of the V. "You're going to be just fine here."

I lifted my drink, and she grabbed hers and clinked mine, making me laugh again.

"So, tell me about you." She steepled her hands beneath her chin.

"Well, how much have they told the town?" I said, resisting the urge to glance around for prying ears. "That I'm a ticking time bomb?"

"Almost nothing. I'm not even sure of your name. You're a mystery girl who blew into town and who the Flynns immediately cloistered. So, naturally, theories abound. But Caoimhe has been talking you up to me every time we run into each other on her way to school. She can't stop talking about how cool you are, but how sad also. And how you need a friend."

Keev, you conniving, meddling kid, I thought, feeling my smile tighten. I couldn't decide in that moment whether I should feel endeared by or angry at her meddling.

"Don't do that," she said sharply and pointed a finger in my face, making me jump. "Don't think I'm only here because of her. I swear I was intrigued long before that. I just didn't have an *in*, until running into you today. I've wanted to know the real story since you got here."

"How much time do you have?" I joked with an eyeroll. The few sips of whiskey made it far easier to brush off these mixed emotions than usual.

"We have all the time, hun. Start with the little stuff. Where you grew up, what you want to do, favorite band, et cetera. We're going to be friends for a long time. There's no need to rush into the heavy stuff."

"You're so certain of that?" I scoffed with a small incredulous laugh. The conviction in her voice was so innocent and genuine. "I've barely said fifty words."

"Yeah, but I just know." She shrugged, smirking. "I've had this feeling for a while now, like someone important was coming. I had the same feeling a little before I met my husband and just before we got pregnant. It's gotten stronger ever since you came to town, but it wasn't until running into you today that I *knew*. Trust me, we're going to be friends. Initially, I keep you from self-destructing, then I help you learn the 'control' you want. And you'll be best friends with my daughter too..." She trailed off, as if realizing she was getting ahead of herself.

She shook her head and waved a hand absently. "It gets vaguer the more I lean into it, but that's the gist."

"Are you...are you a seer?" I asked, stumbling over the vocabulary. I only knew the barest basics of how our magic worked, thanks to the books that had mysteriously arrived on our doorstep, but reading them was slow going. I found myself wanting to disappear into fiction more than learning boring history. But from my cursory research, I'd gathered that seers were common in ancient times, but today they were rare. As rare, if not rarer, than elementals like me.

"No, not really." She waved her hand again. "True Sight is diminished to intuition. But I get flashes, like quick snapshots into the future—my future only. And I see you through a lot of those flashes, as I get older, as my daughter gets older..."

"Doesn't it make you want to act against it? Do the opposite of what the future wants you to do?" I asked, frowning. If fate told me to be friends with someone, I imagined I'd resent the person instead.

"Sometimes, yeah," she said with a laugh. "But something as benign as this? I think, where's the harm?"

Well, I can't argue with that. If fate wants to give me a friend in my hour of need, I'm not going to bite that hand.

"I'm Danielle," I said after a moment. "I'm from Colorado. I just want to get back on track to be a makeup artist. And my favorite band is too big of a question for tonight."

"I'm Aoife." She raised her glass in a salute. "A healer. Raised here, went to school in Dublin, where I met my husband Declan. He's in the band, Killer Craic, that's about to play."

We talked until the show started, then we crowded right up against the stage with the rest of the audience. For the next hour there was only loud music, lights, and a concert atmosphere that I missed. I felt truly alive for the first time in months. The show was over too soon, though, and Aoife snuck me out of the venue ahead of the rest of the crowd.

I thought she was walking me back to the Flynns, and I was leaning toward embracing their wrath and just walking through the front door rather than sneaking back in half-drunk. But Aoife turned a different way and told me she was taking me to *her* house because she still had something else to talk to me about. I doubt I hid my relief at hearing I didn't have to return to my cloistered den just yet.

"I should warn you," she said as we walked up to her small house. "My daughter is a stubborn one, and she insists on staying up until we get home from these shows. She forces herself to nap extra long so she can stay awake, and we and the babysitter have completely given up the fight on this one. So you'll get to meet my Libby!"

My feet almost froze on the porch step beneath me. I didn't know how old she was, but Aoife'd implied she was young like Colt, my nephew who'd died with the rest of my family. My grief was still so volatile that I had no idea how I'd react if I saw a kid his age.

But I didn't know how to politely say that I didn't want to meet her kid. So instead, I made my feet keep moving, following her, as dread coursed down my legs to my toes.

She let me into her house and called out to her daughter. I squeezed my eyes closed when I heard a squeal and skittering footsteps from the back of the house and didn't realize I'd backed against the wall until my shoulder blades touched it and I nearly jumped out of my skin. The pounding of my pulse sounded like waves in my eardrums, but it didn't cover their voices, spewing loving gibberish at each other.

"Libby baby, this is Mommy's new friend Danielle," Aoife said, and my heart sank.

Please, please be older than Colt. But I could tell from the sounds what I was about to be confronted with. This was going to be bad. I took a deep breath and opened my eyes.

The small child in her arms was a tiny child version of her mother, with her dark blond hair tied back into neat braids and huge blue eyes. She hunched in her mom's arms, away from me, suddenly shy.

The bubble of elation that had been carrying me just above the surface of grief all night burst violently. She was the same size and the same age as Colt. My eyes filled with tears, and through them, Libby's blond little head warped into my nephew's brown skin and dark curls.

The sob that ripped from my throat was deafening to my ears, and through my swimming vision, I saw the Cronenberg-like Libby-Colt toddler shrink into her mother's neck. I forced my eyes closed, and my hand to my mouth. I wasn't sure how long I shook and cried or exactly when the floor came up to meet my knees. And I was only distantly aware that I was making an embarrassing scene in front of a practical stranger and her daughter. All I felt was the pain whistling through the ragged holes in my heart where the people I loved used to sit.

Finally, after who knew how long, a little hand patted my knee. I opened my eyes slowly and focused on her little face. It had reverted back from its grief-induced distortion to the small cherub face of a pale child with neat, dark blond braids. Her blue eyes were huge with wariness, but when they met mine, her little smile curved up into a sad, almost *knowing* smile.

Without asking or prompting, she climbed between my knees and tucked herself into my chest, snaking her little arms around my neck. I was scared to embrace her at first, too afraid my grief would make me squeeze her too hard and frighten her. But when she nuzzled her face into my collarbone, instinct took over, and my arms wrapped around her little body with just the right amount of strength.

I was able to take a long, ragged breath finally and let it out in a whistling gust into her hair. The pain in my heart was still there, but it was less of a stabbing pain and more of an ache. An ache that felt almost good.

MARCH

CHAPTER 7

FELKYN

S tepping out of the label office lobby into Italian sunlight in late winter was jarring, and it took me a second to adjust. I was used to sunlight in this hemisphere meaning *heat*, but in late March, the weather still had a Mediterranean chill to it.

I'd just wrapped up a meeting with Lorenzo and the recording team. The finishing touches were almost complete on my song, and I would no longer be needed for recording. I would be back to hear the final version, but my part in the process was complete. The song was set to release in the next month or two.

It would drop a few months shy of the year mark, much to my chagrin. I'd pushed—just short of *begged*—for the release date to be at the year mark for my reunion with Danielle, but the label didn't budge. They wanted to release the song as soon as possible, before the buzz and shock over the Lonely Vagrants breakup fizzled out. I could have forced their hand with mesmerism to get my way, but I was sick of doing that to Lorenzo and his team. I admired him, and I was tired of screwing him over, and even more, I was tired of messing with his mind.

I was tired of everything really. Missing Danielle had worn me down more than I expected.

She hadn't posted anything to her Instagram in a while. I made a point not to follow her account or like any of her posts, but I lurked. Obsessively, yes, but harmlessly. Mostly she posted pictures of her makeup work on a girl in her early teens, and I could only assume it was the kid of the people she was staying with. The skill Danielle put into her various designs was incredible, and she was slowly getting noticed for it. Occasionally, she was in some of the pictures she posted.

I lived for those posts.

I would stare at her face for what was probably hours, sussing out every emotion in her expression. Whether she looked sad or if there was any hint of real happiness in her smile. The curve to her smile showed she was always embarrassed to be photographed but also coyly proud of her work.

God, I loved her. I missed her. And every thought I had circled back to her.

I paused at my motorcycle, parked at the curb. I had several motorcycles in garages across the globe in my favorite cities for driving, since it was nearly impossible to shift with a motor vehicle. This one was the same as the one that now sat in the ocean, beneath the cliff I'd been thrown off. It was my main cycle and my most loved, because I had to be in Italy so much for recordings, meetings, and publicity stuff.

But I won't need it much longer, will I? I mused sadly.

My time in the music business was all but complete, and I'd have to fade completely into obscurity. I'd known this day would come, but I'd selfishly prolonged it with this solo single. Riley hadn't approved, and, hell, part of me didn't approve either, but I'd needed to get the words out and then it practically demanded to be put out into the world. Consequences be damned.

I tossed the keys back and forth between my hands, debating what to do with my evening. I was in the mood for a cliffside, dirt road kind of drive. If I filled my tank, I could just make it up to the old homestead and back to the nearest petrol station. It was a gorgeous cliffside drive, with a breathtaking view of the blue ocean on one side.

Halfway out of downtown, I paused on my bike and pulled over. What'd caught my eye was a huge illuminated marquee on the border of a huge stadium. It showed the poster image of a popular American emo punk band playing there that night, but I'd stopped because it listed Killer Craic as their opener.

Good for them. They deserve this. I smiled up at the marquee with a prideful grin. I'd loved how their sound perfectly mixed Flogging Molly with Avenged Sevenfold and how comfortably unambitious the band was. Yet here they were, opening for such a big band in *Milan*. I had to see this.

I pulled my bike into the long line of traffic queuing for the parking garage, itching with secondhand excitement, almost as if *I* were the one about to be performing. Once parked, I shifted directly inside the venue, beyond the ticketing line and security, and stashed my helmet behind a pile of boxes in the merch booth.

I peeked inside the arena and stood at the top of a set of stairs way in the back of the stands, looking down at the stage far below. God, I missed performing and the atmosphere around a concert: everything from the fans to the bustle of the stage crew. To be down there again would be such a treat. But I couldn't. Not until enough time had passed out of respect for Colin and Riley, and not until I found a new band, which sounded exhausting.

Satisfied, I backed out into the concession hallway and wandered among the crowd. Dodging lines for merch, arena food, and drinks, I found an area of annex hallway that was less densely populated, near the seats with obstructed views. Knowing there were probably unsold seats in that section, I started to head into the stands, but I paused as I caught a glimpse of a brunette in my peripheral.

Jeez, man you have a serious problem, I chided myself as my feet froze at the mere idea that it was Danielle in the corner of my eye.

But it *was* her.

She stood at the less-crowded bar, facing the bartender and comparing the menu to the tablet in her other hand. She frowned at the two, concentrating hard and mouthing to herself. I was far away, but my Lapsi hearing picked up on her ordering two drinks in nearly perfect Italian. She smiled when the bartender complimented her for her effort.

That smile. I swayed on my feet at the sight of it but stopped myself before the movement could catch her attention. I stayed still, and out of her view, holding my breath unnecessarily.

She waited for her drinks in her quiet, pretty way that'd first drawn me in. Her hair fell in neat layers to below her collarbones, and she'd dyed her vibrant streaks back to her natural medium brown. She wore a denim jacket, a band T-shirt, and denim shorts over fishnet tights. I bit my bottom lip to keep my tongue from flicking out at the sight of the fishnets. Was she wearing them for the emo style or to cover the pink scars that marked the length of her legs? Either way, I was a fan.

I couldn't believe she was here. But even more, I couldn't believe I hadn't *felt* her. I'd fed from her once, which meant I'd be able to feel her if we were in the same room. It was a defense mechanism that alerted us to familiar prey. It wasn't a scent, exactly, but a mild buzz on the skin. Yet here she was, and nothing had warned me.

She tucked the tablet into her bag when her drinks were ready, then grinned at the bartender and thanked him in Italian. I ducked out of sight as she passed my hiding space, then, despite knowing I shouldn't, I followed. She stopped at a door, and the security guard pushed it open for her. As she walked backward through it, thanking him, the badge she wore on a lanyard around her neck flashed in the light. Was she working for the band, or was she a guest?

I should've left, but my curiosity was a pushy, sultry temptress. So instead of vanishing, I shifted backstage, where they'd partitioned off areas of the arena floor for various purposes. It was bustling, and I was immediately out of place in my faded jeans and light grey V-neck, but with minimal magical effort, I gently persuaded the minds nearby to ignore me.

I wandered carefully for a bit until I found Danielle again, in an open space converted into a secondary green room for the openers. She handed one drink to a beautiful curvy blonde and set her own down on a side table and bent down.

"Hey, you!" she said, clapping and holding her arms out. A small child ran toward her, dark blond waves creased by a heavy set of noise-canceling headphones around her neck. She squealed as Danielle lifted her into her arms and stood up straight. "Are you ready to see Daddy play?"

"This place is huge!" the girl said, awed.

"Yes, it is! It's the biggest venue yet! And it's going to be *loud*. So you know what to do?"

"Headphones," she said, patting the bulky things around her neck with her small hands.

"Yes, headphones! And you don't take them off for anything, right?" The girl nodded and Danielle lifted her higher while she squealed.

The child's foot caught in the folds of Danielle's T-shirt, pulling it upward. It drew my eye as it exposed a large white bandage covering her abdomen. It could have been covering a fresh tattoo, or it could be an injury. I didn't know, and I couldn't ask.

Despite my concern, I turned away from the doorway, ready—yet not ready—to disappear before I was discovered. But I turned directly into Declan.

"Woah, man, it *is* you!" Declan said, smiling at me, even while I pulled him away from the door, praying the people inside hadn't seen me or heard him.

"Hey..." I said with a wane, uncomfortable smile. "You, woah, you grew out your hair. I thought you were bald..."

"Ha, no, it was just for the image, but being a dad is finally sinking in, and I'm embracing it."

"And you wear glasses? The façade is ruined," I joked softly, guiding us a few more feet from the green room and praying Danielle didn't emerge. "Hey, congrats on this, man. This is huge!"

"Thank you, and thank *you*, I hear you put in a good word," Declan said. "This has been exhausting but amazing. Are you here for the show?"

"You bet, man," I said the half-lie enthusiastically. This wasn't a planned visit. I waved in the general direction of those side seats with poor visibility that weren't filled. "I'll be up there, somewhere, out of the way."

"Nonsense, watch from back here," he said with a wave. He looked past me at the doorway I'd been lurking by. "Does Danielle know you're here? She'll be so surprised—"

"No, no. I'm not here, okay?" I said quickly, holding my hands up. But my mind was working overtime analyzing his tone and whether it suggested she'd be a *good* surprised or an angry surprised. "I didn't know she would be here, and she can't know I'm here."

He looked like he was about to protest, but my terrified face must have stopped him because he nodded.

"How do you, uh, know Danielle?" I asked carefully, lowering my voice when saying her name, worried she'd somehow hear it even though we were out of earshot. "Is she working for you, or what?"

"She's my wife's best mate, and they're coming to some of our bigger shows," he explained. "As far as working for us, nah. But maybe the headliner will use her for little things down the line. They're already impressed with her. She's great, really."

"Yeah, she really is," I agreed, thinking of her growing Instagram portfolio. This was what I'd hoped for her. Work, travel, and friends. She was spreading her wings. I could relax a little, knowing this. "And *how* is she?"

"Oh, I don't really know, mate," he answered with a shrug. "I've been busy with show stuff whenever I see her. I'm not the best insight into how she is. My wife is. But I'm sure if you go in there, she'll be happy to see you."

"I can't. I'm not really here," I murmured, looking back at the door, worried she'd come out any second. I turned back to Declan.

"Whatever you say. But I have to get a good luck hug from my daughter and kiss my wife."

"Sure, sure. But, Declan, *this conversation didn't happen*," I told him, pressing also to wipe the past few minutes from his mind. I felt gross doing it, but I couldn't risk him telling Danielle he'd seen me.

He disappeared into the room, and even though I really didn't want to, I shifted away from backstage. I stood in the stands and watched Declan's band open. But I only stayed for a few songs. Knowing I was within yards of Danielle was too tempting. I left before my willpower broke.

MAY

CHAPTER 8

DANIELLE

"**G**irl, I should have followed your lead and stayed out there between the tour and the festival," Shauna sighed on the other end of the line.

"Yeah, you should've. I'd have loved the company," I mumbled, too tired to put the proper emphasis on the words. I meant it though. I perched my phone between my ear and shoulder and leaned my hands on the counter of the little kitchenette while I watched the coffee slowly percolate into my mug.

"But instead, I got all settled back at home, and almost immediately, my butt was back on a plane." She huffed loudly for effect. "I swear, Danielle, I'm getting too old for this."

"You're twenty-eight," I reminded her, rolling my eyes. I tapped the top of the coffee maker, as if it would make the dinky thing brew faster. "But, you know, just say the word and you can sit this one out. I'll step in and rock this."

"Ha! And we both know you would," she agreed with a chuckle. "But that's something you should've suggested twenty hours ago, before I got on the goddamn plane in L.A."

I shuddered at the thought of traveling for twenty hours. I'd done it once before, and I couldn't fathom doing it numerous times a year. The band was comfortable in business class, but the staff were in economy.

"And you're *sure* you want to go out tonight? After two long flights, that'd be the last thing I'd want to do."

It *had* been the last thing I'd wanted to do. We'd gotten to the hotel in Rome and crashed for hours, until Raymond got stir-crazy and dragged us to his favorite places. *Shit, that was almost a year ago*, I realized, and the pang in my chest made me nearly drop the phone.

"Hell yeah! I slept on the plane." I pictured her waving off my concern with a flick of her hand. "Tonight, we party, tomorrow, we work, and for the rest of it, we enjoy a music festival full of the best fucking bands on the planet! Then I can relax, go back home, and *stay there.*"

"Yeah, and I'll have to figure out what I'm going to do," I mumbled, not entirely meaning to say it out loud.

"Pffft, you have *excellent* references now," she said, and again I could imagine her waving my worry away. "And don't worry. We're not leaving you hanging."

"What does that mean?" I asked, my brows coming together. That sounded a little too purposefully vague.

She didn't answer me though. She started barking irritably at someone about luggage and not running someone down. She sounded muffled, like she'd pulled the phone away from her face to berate one of our various backstage coworkers traveling with her—probably Bentley.

"We're nearing the tram for baggage claim. But Cody's disappeared somewhere, and we need all the hands for the bags..." she rambled, talking to me again.

"But aren't you glad you have so much less to haul this time, since you left all your shit with *me* to schlepp to the festival..." I chided her, eyeing the stack of black cases in the corner, which

I'd had to maneuver there by myself from the airport a week and a half ago. "Enjoy it now, because you're taking all this back with you. It's not my job anymore after tomorrow."

She said something in a haughty tone, but it cut out every other word. When the sound returned to normal, music blared from her side of the phone, like she was passing right under a speaker. It was a slow song, and I heard violins.

"What was that?" I demanded, surprised by the urgency in my voice. Something in the melody tugged at me. I tried to listen harder for more, but it was too soft now. She'd moved away.

"Oh, some new...by..." Her voice cut in and out again.

"By who? I didn't catch that," I said, still straining to listen, but she was barking orders at our coworkers again. *Oh well*, I shrugged. The tune was already out of my head.

"The tram's here. I should get off the phone and let you go. One more thing, you're sure we can check in early?"

"Yes, I triple checked with the concierge. We're not the only convoy coming through early, and they're ready for us—you. I've been here." I stirred creamer into my coffee, now that it was finally done brewing.

"Thank you, rock star! You're the best!" she said.

I had nothing to do with it, though. It was all scheduled weeks ago through the tour logistics department. I just happened to be there because I'd asked them to book me a week and a half early, on my dime.

"Just get here, get settled, and crash for a bit. I'm going to go for a run," I told her, sitting on the side of my bed and rubbing my eyes.

"A *run*?" she scoffed.

"Yeah, a run. *You* got me up at this ungodly hour," I grumbled, glaring at the digital clock on the nightstand as it changed from 8:28 to 8:29. "I can't go back to sleep. So I'm going to go for a jaunty jog, then it's laundry day."

"So exciting," she teased, sounding distracted. Someone in the background made some kind of joke and she snorted. "Well, have fun with that. I'll text you when we get to the hotel, but no need to meet me in the lobby or anything."

We hung up, and I flopped back onto the bed, draping my arms across my eyes. Eight in the morning wasn't atrociously early, if you were normal, but I couldn't remember the last time I'd seen this side of ten a.m. I lay there for another minute before getting back up and taking my coffee over to the seat by the window. While the caffeine worked through my system, I stared out at the quaint streets of Antwerp, Belgium.

At the start of the tour, I'd been traveling with Aoife and Libby to the bigger shows in touristy cities. We'd see Declan and the headliner perform, then stay an extra day or two and be tourists before heading back to Ireland for a few days. We'd been to Milan, Edinburgh, Berlin, Strausburg, and from there I lost track.

At the tail end of the tour, Shauna, the lead makeup artist for the headlining band, fell terribly ill. I was pulled out of the greenroom, given the briefest but most intense job interview in history, during which they tried to terrify me into thinking the bandmates were the most difficult divas. But I'd barely blinked. Jeremy had taught me how to let attitude roll off my back better than any high school drama kid ever had.

They'd been messing with me, to see if I panicked, but I passed. I covered the whole night by myself and impressed them so much that they offered me a job as Shauna's assistant—basically a glorified brush cleaner and errand girl.

At first, Shauna chaffed at the idea of an assistant because she thought it superfluous. She would have terrified the old me, but I stubbornly held my ground around her, showing an eagerness to please—but not kiss ass—and quickly broke down her walls.

From there, she treated it more as a mentorship and showered me with insight into the industry and how to go after the kind of work I wanted. She told me, like with many things, it was a matter of luck and who you knew, and she was adamant that *this* was my foot in the door.

I traveled full time with the band after that, staying in hotels or traveling overnight with the rest of the staff. The job barely paid anything, but travel, lodging, and food was covered within the tour's budget. The experience was payment enough.

It was simultaneously exhausting, thrilling, and lax. The bustle of the job was only for six hours out of every forty-eight. The rest of it was boring travel, partying, and jetlag. If we didn't have back-to-back days of shows, we often went out afterward and didn't crawl into bed until three or four in the morning. It had been the best time of my life.

Technically, the tour ended over a week ago, and Declan's band had returned home to Bray. But I was contracted for one last event they attached to the end of their tour. Groezrock was a three-day music festival in Belgium, one of the biggest punk rock festivals in the world. They were one of the larger performances on the first day of the festival, which tomorrow.

Staying in Belgium between the tour's end and the festival burned a decent chunk of my pre-abduction savings, but I didn't care. Anything was better than going back to the Flynns for the week and a half. I loved Caoimhe like a sister, but her parents were on my last nerves.

Their generosity was always at such odds with their animosity toward me. And when they asked about the places I'd been, they always found different ways to ask if I still wore the damn bracelet—I did—or if I'd been in contact with anyone from my past or anyone from *that band*. Even though the answer to *that* question was always an adamant no, I tried to skirt around it because it was none of their business.

I was looking forward to the festival, but it meant I had to figure out what I was going to do *after*. I wasn't ready to go back to the states yet, and though I missed Aoife, Libby, and Caoimhe, I would go insane if I stayed in Bray more than a few days.

What I'd give to just keep traveling. I liked it more than I ever expected to. I was just a "shop girl" from Colorado, who never thought she'd leave her own country, but now I'd lost count of how many stamps were in my passport.

I finished my coffee, washed the mug in the bathroom sink, then quickly changed into my last pair of clean leggings, socks, and a not-so-clean T-shirt. Making sure I had my keycard, ID, and precious iPod all secured in my pockets, I left the hotel room for my daily run.

I'd thought it would be daunting, traveling to so many new places, but—and I hate that I owe anything to *him* or the monsters that destroyed my life—my experiences over the past year had evaporated any kind of trivial fear of the unknown.

It took me a while to realize it, because I'd been reeling from tragedy and grief, but after facing death numerous times at the hands of immortal supernatural beings, things like a boss's ego or being thrust into a new living situation seemed arbitrary. I'd really only let the Flynns push me around at the beginning because of the depression and the hopelessness I'd felt in the situation.

Aoife had dug me out of that depression and carried me away to new places. I'd caught my foot in the door to my career. And for the first time in I didn't know how long, I felt a shred of optimism.

But I wasn't fooled into thinking that my depression—as well as the debilitating grief—was gone. They weren't going anywhere, and there'd been times during this week and a half that had severely humbled me.

Did I have a good, long, hysterical cry while on a run through a quiet cemetery because an intrusive thought made me imagine my family was in there? Yep.

Later, after I recovered from those hysterics, did I suddenly go into a panic, trying to remember whether my family was even buried anywhere or if they were somehow waiting for *me* to arrange it? Yupperoony.

Did I call anywhere to reassure myself that they were, in fact, all laid to rest in some form or fashion? No. I couldn't bring myself to check.

And how many times in the past week and a half had I almost called Felkyn? Less than in my first few weeks with the Flynns, but still not zero.

But today was different. Today the depression wouldn't catch me. Today was laundry day, and then friends were coming back into my life and bringing chaos with them. And I couldn't wait.

CHAPTER 9

DANIELLE

"So, Danielle, I see you gave up on the bangs already," Bentley called over his shoulder from the head of the pack. "They didn't look that bad, you know."

I rolled my eyes at the back-handed compliment, but the buzz from the last round hadn't worn off yet, so I couldn't hold onto my irritation for long. Instead, I scoffed a little and grumbled behind everyone else.

I'd impulsively given myself bangs a few weeks ago, shortly after being hired. It was something I did when I felt a lot of change happening: I changed something about myself to feel in control. Most often it was hair-related, but other times it was a tattoo or burning myself to get rid of the words magically carved into my abdomen. This time, it'd been bangs. I instantly regretted it, but thankfully I hadn't sheared them too short and my hair grew quickly. A few weeks in headbands and barrettes, and already I could tuck most of the short layers behind my ears.

"Yeah, no more bangs for me. That's the last time I impulsively cut my hair for a while—I hope," I called up to him. His shoulders shook with an exaggerated, silent laugh.

"A shame. I like a girl with bangs," he said, and while he didn't turn, I could feel his smirk from several feet back.

Bentley was twenty-four and the *bro* of the group, which was at odds with his working for an emo band. He was the muscle, hauling equipment around the stage, organizing the miles of cables, and loading the buses.

"More like you like girls that bang," Geoff said out of the side of his mouth. It was a snide comment meant only for the guys up front to hear, but we were all bordering on drunk, so everything came out louder than intended.

Ugh, yes, make fun of the virgin in the group, I thought but thankfully didn't say aloud. Instead I hummed the tune of Bowling for Soup's "High School Never Ends" to myself and followed behind them. Sadie snickered next to me.

"Lay off her, *Bentley*," Shauna snapped at him. She punched him in the shoulder with more force than a friendly swat. "Or the next *two* rounds are on you."

"Ugh, can the next bar be one with more seating? Or maybe a patio? My feet hurt..." Sadie complained quietly.

I directed us to a cozy bar with an outdoor patio that I'd passed a few times while running.

"Good find, scout," Geoff said when we arrived at this low-key bar. He nudged my arm with his elbow, buddy-buddy-like, even though he'd joked about me being a prude just minutes ago. "Bentley, I believe it's your turn, right?"

"Yeah, yeah, what's everyone getting?" Bentley grumbled.

We agreed on a round of cheap bourbons, and he went off with another guy to fetch it. Shauna and Sadie settled gratefully into seats on the patio, while others milled around. I stood with Clay, Derek, and Geoff by a lit outdoor fireplace.

"I know he's a bit of a bully, but damn," Clay murmured to the three of us after Bentley passed us our drinks and walked away. He stared after Bentley, practically drooling. "Never thought I'd like 'em mean, but I'm a sucker for broad shoulders and dark hair."

"Not my type at all," I said with a scoff. I took a sip from the tumbler, and heat spread over my tongue. Without warning, I blurted, "I prefer blonds."

"Noted," Derek, the only blond in the group, said with a lopsided grin that bordered on flirty.

I was opening my mouth to turn the conversation somewhere else when a song played behind me. I'd heard the same tune earlier when on the phone with Shauna. This time, it was louder, clearer, and accompanied by a drawn-out vocal that shot electricity down my spine and wrapped a hand around my heart. I whirled around, looking for the source.

My eyes fell on Shauna, her phone in her hand. Eyeing me with surprise, she pressed the screen and the song stopped. I stormed over to her.

"Woah, Danielle, you okay?" Derek called after me.

"What was that?" I demanded from Shauna. I knew *whose* voice it'd been, but I didn't recognize the tune from any of their released songs. "I know all their songs. That wasn't Lonely Vagrants."

"No, it's a new solo single," Sadie said, looking up at me with big drink-clouded eyes. "Just by Felkyn. It came out this week."

"He put out a solo..." I meant it as a question, but the words tumbled from my lips in an awed murmur. "I need to hear it."

"Why are you *so* intense right now?" Geoff said, coming up behind me.

"Woah, wait," Bentley cut in, looking like he saw me in a new light. "Are you *that* Danielle?"

Shit. I felt all their eyes on me. I raked a hand through my hair, pulling my short layers forward to subtly obscure my face, even though my face had never been in the tabloids—well, it *had*, but for the kidnapping aspect, not for the *band* drama.

"She did say she prefers blonds," Geoff mumbled to Derek.

Fuck. I needed to think fast, but the buzz made it harder.

"Am I *what* Danielle?" I demanded, looking as confused as I could. I sat down heavily in the seat next to Shauna, still shaking my head so my hair fell forward, but I tried to catch her eye.

"The girl from the song," Sadie insisted softly.

"The one that broke them up!" Clay piped up.

"*They broke up*?" I practically yelled it, theatrically pretending it was the most horrifying news I'd ever heard. "What the *fuck*? *When*?"

"Like a year ago."

"Where have you *been*?"

"Too busy fucking Felkyn to notice apparently." That one was Bentley. "I bet that's how she got this job."

"Why *else* wouldn't they be at Groezrock?"

I pretended like I didn't hear any of their comments and was still in a state of horrified shock. Real tears welled in my eyes before I could stop them, but they added to the effect.

"This is...this is the worst thing I've ever heard." I turned to Shauna, who still held her phone flat in her hand, dumbstruck. I pulled my iPod out of my bag and unwound my headphones. "I need to hear this song *right now*. Can I see your phone?"

"Why don't you use yours?" someone asked.

"Because I don't have any kind of data plan," I admitted, not looking up at them, while Shauna passed me her phone and I plugged my headphones into it.

"What!?"

"Why don't you have a data plan?"

They were almost more horrified at that admission than the earlier suggestion I was *that* Danielle. They'd never understand that being constantly connected to social media was triggering, so I kept everything on airplane mode until I needed to download more books.

Instead of answering them, I shoved my headphones into my ears, set the song back to the beginning, and hit play. I hunched over the phone, cupping my ears to shut them all out.

The first notes tugged at my heart, but it practically tore at the seams when his voice started: a long, drawn-out vibrato. He hadn't been the frontman and only sang the backup vocals, but I'd listened to their music so much while living with them and in the year afterward that I could pick his voice out in every song.

Then the lyrics started, and by the first chorus, a sob rose in my throat that I barely kept down.

It was a slow, hauntingly beautiful ballad that built in intensity into the chorus, but just before reaching any kind of final, satisfying crescendo, it just...stopped, and the next verse started again, slow and sad, but hopeful.

Fuck, Felkyn...I thought when the violins started in the bridge, mirroring the cadence of the chorus. I pressed my legs tighter together and forgot where I was for the moment. The violin always did me in.

The song ended with one last chorus, this one slower and more drawn out, until the song, like each chorus, ended abruptly, leaving the listener—me—unsatisfied.

I sat silently for a moment after the song ended, emotionally wrung out but simultaneously exhilarated. The song itself wasn't heartbreaking but heart-tugging. Yet it felt like mine was shredded. I missed him, and I wanted him there. I needed him there.

I pulled my headphones out and handed the phone back to Shauna. I looked up at everyone else, and their expressions ranged from judgmental to sympathetic. I rubbed my eyes, and they came away wet.

"So, is it about you?" Sadie asked softly, leaning across Shauna's lap so I could hear her.

"What? No," I said, my voice thick, but I shook my head adamantly and shot to my feet. "It's just beautiful. Jeez."

I chaffed from the attention and swiped at my eyes again to make sure more tears weren't coming. I found my drink on the arm of the chair where I'd left it and quickly downed it.

"Hey, give her some air," Shauna said defensively, getting to her feet behind me.

"Someone get her another drink," one of the guys said.

"No, no. I mean, air, yes. Air sounds good," I mumbled, sidestepping all of them. "I think I'll head back to the hotel."

I couldn't stay there. I needed out from under their gazes and to process what I'd just heard and how I felt about it.

"What? No, don't go yet," Clay said when I passed him. He stepped in front of me so I had to stop. "The night's still young. We have more drinks to drink."

"My mood's gone, I'm afraid."

"Because of a song?"

"*Yes*," I said in a sputter, shaking my head to hide that I was rapidly blinking away tears. I sniffed and stepped around him. "I just found out my favorite band broke up. *And* I just heard the most beautiful song in the world. I need to go lie in my feels about it! I'll see you all tomorrow."

I didn't wait to hear anyone's response and speedwalked out of the bar. I needed to get out of there fast because my heart was breaking open and I wasn't entirely sure what was going to come pouring out.

Back in my room, I dropped my things on the bed and paced around the small room, a mess of conflicting emotions. One thing I knew for certain was I needed more to drink. Whether to drown my sudden sorrows or awaken more, I didn't know. But I stomped to the cupboard where I kept my meager food supply and pulled out the cheap bottle of wine I hadn't opened yet. I unscrewed the top and took an ambitious swig, then carried it with me to the bed.

My phone was buzzing with a call, and I nearly spat out my second mouthful of wine in my panic, thinking it was *him* calling. But it was only Shauna. She'd called three times, apparently, while I was retreating back to the hotel. I rejected the call and shot her a quick text before putting my phone on do not disturb.

Made it back safe. I'm fine. Just having some big feels. Hope I still have a job tomorrow!?

Another sip of wine, straight from the bottle. I looked down at my phone again and nearly choked. My traitorous fingers had pulled up Felkyn's contact, and my thumb hovered over the green call button. With a squeal, I tossed the phone away from me and hugged the bottle to my chest.

My jean shorts suddenly felt too restrictive, and so did my top and my shoes.

Maybe a shower would be good. And maybe another listen to the song. Because I'm ever the masochist.

The room swayed when I stood, but only a little. I took my tablet and Bluetooth speaker with me and stripped gracelessly on my way to the bathroom, where I turned the water on as hot as I could. While it got up to temp, I pulled up the song again and set it to play on loop with the volume all the way up—the whole floor was booked for my coworkers who were still out on the town, so I didn't have to worry about keeping anyone awake. With a shaky breath, I hit play and ducked beneath the hot stream.

In the privacy of my shower, the song hit differently because I was able to better focus on the words and not just the chorus and the instruments.

The first verse expressed how he first fell when I stood up for myself while my world was crumbling around me. I remembered it well: I lost my shit at Jeremy, and after, Felkyn sat outside the bathroom, merely keeping me company while I put myself back together.

The second and third verses were similar, subtle callbacks to our short but impactful time together. In each chorus, he promised to stand back while I blew the world away but protect me when I couldn't protect myself. As the chorus built, about to break, he promised he'd always be there, even when I chose to walk away. But then the chorus broke, in that unsatisfying way, with the line "But 'til then, I'll wait..."

By the third time through the song, I was hugging my knees and sobbing on the floor of the bathtub.

Damn it, Felkyn, I was doing fine, I fumed silently at him. I'd been doing fine enough—still missing him and still depressed, yeah, but fine—and now I was crying in the shower, ready to break my promise to myself and call him.

With one song, he'd cut me open and pointed a giant, glaring spotlight down on the mess I'd made of myself.

I'd sent him away to basically spin my wheels for a year. I'd spiraled. I'd let myself be bullied into submission. I'd simply sunk beneath the waves, when I could have had someone there the whole time to hold me and tell me I was strong. He would have simply made it easier to face the waking world.

He was right in his song, though. From the beginning, I'd been piecing myself back together, *alone*, but just *liked* him being there. He'd never imposed when he knew I could handle it—in fact, he loved to see me handle it. He only stepped in to protect me when it was something I physically couldn't do myself; otherwise, he stood back.

I was better with him backing me up and offering a hand when I needed it. This whole year he could have been my raft in the ocean.

But that wasn't fair to Aoife. I wouldn't have met her if I hadn't gone my own way. She'd pulled me out while I was drowning in despair, and she filled a spot in my heart left by Alexis. Caoimhe filled the spot of my sister—albeit the younger sister I'd never had. Libby filled the spot of Colt, my nephew. And Declan had pulled me into the music world.

Yes, I'd pushed Felkyn away. Yes, I'd struggled to find my footing, but I'd pushed through, found a friend, a family, a job.

And not just a job, but one that opened doors into the career I'd always wanted.

If I hadn't left him, I'd have struggled less. The footing would be surer beneath my feet, because he'd build a pedestal beneath me, a brick at a time. If it shook, he'd catch me. I'd never fall, and he wouldn't rest until he saw me *fly*.

But I wouldn't have met Aoife, I wouldn't have healed the parts of myself that were semi-healed now. Would I be more healed, less healed, or just different?

Maybe the chips were always meant to fall this way.

But 'til then, I'll wait...

Eventually I got out of the shower, toweled off, and dressed in an oversized T-shirt. I continued to pace my apartment, drinking more and more wine straight from the bottle. Round and round my thoughts circled, volleying between regretting my choices; being grateful I'd made them; regretting leaving Felkyn; being grateful I'd met Aoife, Caoimhe, Libby, Declan, and Shauna; saying fuck it and pulling myself back from that edge.

I didn't have to decide tonight. He would respect our agreement until the year was up, and if after that I still didn't want to see him, he'd respect it. But damn it, I already knew I wanted him.

He'll wait.

I could wait.

I didn't want to wait.

The phone was in my hand. When did that happen? Was it dialing? Did he just answer?

"Fuck." Before I was even sure he'd answered, I hung up.

CHAPTER 10

FELKYN

I was locking the door of my teaching studio when my phone buzzed in my pocket. The phone nearly fell from my fingers when I saw the caller ID, but I held on and only hesitated for a second before answering it.

"He—hello?" I stammered. *Please don't be a pocket dial.*

"Fuck."

It was her voice all right. I might have laughed, if I wasn't so shocked at the suddenness of her call. The line went dead before I could find my voice.

I dropped the phone to my side and sank into an arm chair.

Just a pocket dial. Don't get your hopes up, I chided myself while I perched the phone on my knee. But for a solid three minutes, I stared, unblinking, at the black phone screen, willing it to ring again.

When it did, I snatched it up immediately.

"Danielle?" I said, sounding breathless in my relief that it hadn't been a pocket dial.

It was several beats before she said anything, and the seconds stretched out almost endlessly for me. I tugged on my hair. *Say something. Say anything. Don't hang up.*

I flipped off the lights in the studio and bolted up the stairs to my apartment, praying the whole time that she wouldn't hang up.

"You were supposed to wait a year," she said finally, all in a rush.

"You called me," I teased, then nearly smacked myself. *First time in a year talking to the girl that holds my heart, and I immediately start with teasing.*

"You wrote and released a song!" she snapped quickly, and a little slurred. She sounded drunk, but adorably so. "A little more than *a call*, I'd say."

Ah, she's heard the song. I should have figured as much. It'd been out for a few days, and Lorenzo was ecstatic about the numbers. He wanted a music video, people wanted interviews, TV shows were already asking for the rights to use it. I wanted none of it, but Lorenzo kept trying.

"And you just *assume* it was about you?" I said, smirking, despite my elation at hearing her voice. "That's presumptuous."

"You practically spelled my name out in the lyrics," she pointed out, unamused. I snorted. "The violins were a nice touch. Well played. Poorly timed, though. Because, you know...it's too early."

"It wasn't my idea," I told her honestly. Never mind that I'd been too lazy to argue or be persuasive. "Lorenzo pushed for it to be out ASAP, before people, you know, forgot about LV."

"Trust me, no one's forgotten about LV," she mumbled, as if to herself. "I basically outed myself tonight as *that* Danielle when I heard the song. Way to blindside me."

I sat down heavily on my bed, wincing. All desire to tease her fled. I should have found a way to warn her. I'd have had Riley warn her, but he had me blocked at the moment—forced radio silence. I rubbed my neck and blew out a short sigh.

"I'm sorry. Really I am. It honestly wasn't intentionally manipulative. I hoped you'd hear it, yeah, but...I expected you to still ignore me until the year mark."

I figured your willpower was better than mine, but I'm relieved it wasn't, I almost added but thankfully stopped myself.

"I probably would've, if your song wasn't so devastatingly awesome," she said with a soft sigh. I closed my eyes and could perfectly imagine her shaking her head sadly and begrudgingly.

"I'm still sorry. But...even if it's just to chew me out...it's so good to hear your voice." I was a sap, I knew it. And if I was exposing my bleeding heart for her to tear out, so be it. "I miss you."

"I miss you too," she said, almost too soft for her phone mic to pick up.

"How are you?"

"Uh-uh," she said, after releasing an exasperated huff. "Start with an easier question, please."

"Danielle," I pressed gently, concerned.

"I'm drunk, Felkyn, and unpredictable, and *sad*," she blurted, irritated. "So, unless you want me to unload all my problems onto you in an oversharing rush, try another question."

Of course I want you to unload all your problems onto me. Why wouldn't I want that? I shook my head, bewildered, but held back. She was drunk, and as much as I wanted to know everything about her past ten months, I didn't want to press her. Instead, I shook off my incredulity and relaxed my shoulders. She wasn't going anywhere now that she was done chewing me out. It was a good sign.

"Well, would it be easier if I asked 'what are you wearing?'" I mused, smirking.

"Yeah, actually." She chuckled softly, and I relished the sound. I imagined her sitting on her bed and leaning back onto her elbows as she spoke. "I have no problems telling you what I'm wearing. An oversized T-shirt, and not much else."

In my mind's eye, she lazily extended a bare leg toward the ceiling.

I bit my lip against a grin—as if she could see me. Was I really so basic that *that* alone turned me on?

"I'm sure you look beautiful," I said truthfully, to avoid hinting at how much the simple image aroused me.

"Mmm, hmm. Freshly showered, too," she said cheerfully. Then, aside, she mumbled, "Nothing like a hot shower cry, right?"

"Okay, so how about *where* are you?" I asked, pretending I hadn't heard that but wanting to hug her from here. "Are you still in Ireland?"

I was careful to say *still* in Ireland, even though I knew she'd been traveling. She couldn't know that I'd almost broken our pact by accidentally stalking her at a concert in Milan. I knew the tour was over now, so it was safe to assume she was back in Ireland. She hadn't posted more portfolio pictures of the young teen since the tour, so maybe she'd moved on from Ireland.

"Uh, well, no, actually," she said hesitantly but not irritably. "It's kind of a long story, but I'm actually somewhere else, for, uh, Groezrock."

"Groezrock, really? That's awesome!" We'd performed at the festival the past year, and it had been only our second festival experience. We were slated to return, but then, well, everything happened. Coincidentally, it was while we were attending Groezrock that the Agathati broke into our home and stole Jeremy's daughter, setting everything in motion and leading to meeting Danielle in the first place. *Talk about full circle. I'd love to be there with her.* "It's right up your alley, really. You're in for a lot of great acts."

"Yeah, I'm excited. Tomorrow I'm working it, but after that, I get to enjoy it," she explained. I heard liquid slosh around, like in a glass bottle. I wondered if it was wine or liquor.

"Working it?" My eyebrows drew together. I'd assumed she was attending with friends and I'd interrupted their pre-festival festivities.

"Heh. Yeah. I'm doing the job you casually floated to me last year but couldn't deliver on," she mused.

She named the band, and my head perked up, thrilled at the news. She was *working* working. She'd gotten a makeup job for the headliner of Declan's tour. *Fuck yes!* But before I could exclaim my emphatic congratulations, the sloshing sound of liquid in a bottle stopped, like she'd frozen.

"You didn't have anything to do with this, did you?" she asked slowly, her casual, drunk tone replaced by suspicion. And not playful suspicion.

"What? With what?"

"Bentley said 'I bet that's how she got the job,'" she mumbled to herself. Then, to me, she said, "Felkyn, tell me you didn't pull strings to get me a behind the scenes job..."

"That Bentley guy sounds like an ass," I told her flatly. Then, as calmly and evenly as I could, I said, "Danielle, I wouldn't do that."

I'd had the thought when I saw her at the concert in Milan and might have mentioned it to Declan, but if he was close friends with her, he knew she was capable before I walked on the scene. No, I hadn't done this. She had.

"You didn't make the lead makeup artist sick so they'd ask me?"

"I can't make people sick," I argued, chortling softly.

"You can make people *think* they're sick," she countered. "Or you could have influenced them into hiring me afterward."

"I truly haven't done anything to meddle in your life. I made you a promise," I told her, firmly. "It *sounds* like you lucked into an opportunity and wowed them with pure goddamn talent. Be fucking proud of yourself. You're living your dream."

"Well, I'm inching toward the dream," she corrected me, her words slurred again, now that she wasn't focusing hard on accusing me.

That's right, I thought. I remembered the *dream* was working on a TV show or in theater. But she'd been itching to work with *us* and take full advantage of our inability to sweat.

"Even so, I'm so proud of you," I said. "Fuck Bentley."

"Yeah, fuck him," she agreed with a chuckle. "Mr. I-like-girls-that-bang. No wait, that was Geoff that said that."

"Wow these guys sound like absolute tools," I said with an incredulous huff. "Can I come kick their asses?"

"Much as I'd love to see *that* right now," she said, amused but quite drunk. "It's fine. My petty revenge is *not* sharing my magic hangover cure with them, like I was going to."

"You have magic hangover potions?" I asked with a smirk.

"Not potions exactly, but witchy medicine, yes. Courtesy of Aoife."

"What's an ee-va?"

"Eee-FUH," she said slowly, emphasizing the syllables carefully. "Not to be confused with Caoimhe."

"There's an Eefa *and* a Keeva?"

"Yeah, but don't ask me to spell them right now. I can't on a good day," she said, slurring even more.

"*Dove*, you are *drunk*," I told her with a quiet, exasperated laugh. "And you're not making sense. Please, go take that witchy hangover cure now, before you do worse to yourself."

"I'm fine...but I'll stop for the night and hydrate," she said, sounding like herself again. My sweet, adorable, drunk love. "I should get back inside anyway. Everyone will be coming home soon, and I don't want to be caught outside like this..."

"You're not in your room?" All this time I'd been picturing her lazing on her bed.

"I was, but my pacing got a little out of hand, so I've just been in the hall, and—" She halted so suddenly, I thought the call dropped. "Shit!"

"What?" I demanded, immediately alert.

"Fuck. God damn it," she continued, then let out a long, frustrated sigh. "I'm locked out. Stupid, drunk ass."

"Don't call my beautiful, badass woman stupid," I chided her firmly.

"She might be those things, too, but she also left her damn keycard in the hotel room in the middle of the night and can't get back in," she grumbled. "I know I said I was done drinking, but...one more sip, as punishment."

"Do you want me to come there and let you into your room?" I offered, wincing.

"No. No," she said with a sigh. There was a sliding sound, and I imagined her leaning against her door and sliding down until she was sitting on the floor. Possibly hugging her knees. "They should all be getting back soon. Shauna has my other keycard, in case she had to get her own hangover cure. She'll let me in when they get back. Fuuuuuck!"

She let out another stream of curses and grumbles.

"What?"

"Well, I just remembered...I'm sitting in a hallway, drunk, waiting for my coworkers to get their drunken asses back here...wearing basically just an oversized T-shirt."

"I thought you were messing with me when you said that," I squeezed my eyes closed, feeling her dread secondhand.

"Nope," she squeaked. I heard a dull thump, like she'd dropped her head back against the door. "Fucking great."

"Do you want me to come there and help you?" I asked again, speaking slowly and precisely to emphasize that I was more than willing, she just had to say the word.

"No," she denied again. "Honest to god, no. I...I don't want the first time you see me again to be like *this*. I'd rather be clothed. And not drunk."

But you do *want to see me again?* I desperately wanted to ask whether this was just a one-off drunken conversation because she was sad and had lost control of her resolve, but there was no way to get a sober answer out of her until tomorrow, so I held back.

She took a deep breath and released it slowly, like she was psyching herself up for something.

"It's fine. I've been through far worse," she said as much to me as to herself. "I've got this. Besides, after tomorrow, they aren't coworkers anymore. And while there are still two more days of the festival, I don't have to see the jerks from the group *ever* again if I don't want to."

"Dove, I feel like this is the wrong thing to say in this moment, but your badass is showing, and I adore it," I told her, unable to not smile, imagining her sitting there pepping herself up.

She laughed and grumbled a few more curses to herself. We both fell quiet.

"Dove," she said after a moment.

"What?"

"You've called me *dove*, like, twice."

"I have?" I picked idly at the bedspread, thinking. "I don't know why. I guess I'm a pet name kind of guy, apparently? I don't ever want to call you *baby*. But does *dove* work? Maybe *doveling*?"

Time slowed while I waited for her response.

"I don't hate it," she said after a sultry chuckle. "I was just wondering why *dove*?"

"I don't know. I like birds?" I offered, shrugging. "Though, if we're going with a bird theme, maybe *firebird* is more fitting? Or *phoenix*?"

"Well, I'm not allowed to do the fire stuff, so it's not really fitting, is it?" she muttered under her breath, forgetting I could hear her perfectly.

"What?" I asked, disturbed by the bitterness in her voice.

"Nothing. It doesn't matter," she said airily, as if swatting my concern away with a hand. She sighed. "Dove is fine. I like it. And I like imagining the word on your lips as you lean in to kiss me..."

"Dove..." I said in a low, miserable groan. "You're drunk, so I can't take this all to heart, but..." I trailed off to collect my thoughts, but it was hard. "I've waited ten months to talk to you again..."

"And when you finally got to, I'm a wasted mess," she agreed calmly but sadly. "I'm sorry—"

"No, don't apologize. It's fine. I'm happy to be here in this moment. I love this. I love you. But I...I want to see you. And I want to ask if you want to see me. But even if you say yes...any answer you give..."

She giggled, silencing me because it didn't fit the moment or what I was trying to say.

"One: now you sound like the drunk one," she said, laughter still in her voice. "Two: listening to a mille...millennial...milli-years-old Lapsus grapple with *drunken consent* is more funny than I could have imagined."

I huffed but didn't argue. I could see how it would be funny, but it didn't lessen my frustration.

She cleared her throat. "Here is my drunken ruling." I felt her smirk from here. "I want to see you. Desperately. But not tonight. Let's try tomorrow."

"You work tomorrow."

"Not *all* day. Like three to five in the afternoon. That's all," she said impatiently.

"But how will I know you still want to see me when you're sober?"

"Text me in the fucking morning and ask if it's still okay," she countered with strained patience, probably pinching the bridge of her nose. "But by morning, I mean, like, after ten a.m. I'm not a morning person."

"Will you remember this conversation? If I text you tomorrow, and you don't remember, you're going to hate me for breaking the year pact."

"Fuck you. Give me more credit than that," she snapped. "I'm not *that* drunk, for fuck's sake."

"Yeah? Try standing up right now," I challenged.

"Fuck off," she said, half laughing. "Fine. Take your chances, and don't text me in the morning. If I remember, I'll bitch you out."

"And I'll deserve it," I agreed, admitting defeat. Though was it really defeat? If my heart could beat, it'd be *thrumming*. "But hopefully you'd forgive me."

"After some groveling maybe," she quipped. She breathed in sharply. "Ugh. I can hear them in the elevator. They'll be here in a moment."

"Last offer to save you from this," I told her, silently begging her to just say yes.

"Nope. I'll survive this." I imagined her closing her eyes and mentally preparing herself. "Plus, don't worry about my *virtue*. There are jerks in the group, but there are women who have my back. They're not going to touch me. There's just going to be a lot of 'walk of shame' jokes."

"Dove..." I said once she finished. I could hear them now too, maybe around a corner. She'd probably hang up in a second.

"Hmmm?"

"I love you."

"I love you too." She didn't miss a beat in saying it back.

Part of me still understood that she was drunk and might not mean it in the morning, but the other ninety-five percent of me was doing figurative backflips.

CHAPTER 11

DANIELLE

I t was a wonder I slept at all.

But Aoife's concoction, in addition to preventing miserable hangover symptoms, knocks you out for five hours minimum. I should have been a nervous wreck all night, anticipating seeing Felkyn in the morning, while slowly sobering up and probably vomiting at least four times. Instead, I woke from a dreamless sleep of the dead, with nothing but a terrible case of dry mouth.

My alarm went off at ten, and for once, I had no need to snooze four times before rolling groggily out of bed. Still, though wide awake, I stayed there for a few moments, wondering if I should text him first or wait to see if he chickened out. I couldn't wait though.

I pulled my phone off the charger and, smirking, typed out a message.

> Morning my sunshine beauty, I'm awake and sober. And I have no regrets about last night

I set the phone aside and used the bathroom, then picked my outfit from the freshly folded laundry. I was contemplating fighting with the slow coffee maker when my phone buzzed with an answering text.

I was just about to text you, but couldn't figure out how to say "Please don't hate me, but I'm texting because YOU ASKED ME TO." But you saved me the need. I appreciate it

A beat later, a second message came in.

I like a woman that takes the reins

Don't get used to it. I have absolutely no moves. You can call the shots from here

I absolutely will not

Care to get the awkward reunion out of the way, then join me for Groezrock?

Nothing between us has ever been awkward. We're rockstars together

I snorted and rolled my eyes.

> I'd love to. Text me the hotel and the room number

I responded with the details, then glanced between the clothes on the bed, my still-bare legs, and the coffee maker that took forever. He wasn't coming here immediately, was he? I sent off another text to ask when to expect him.

> I just need about an hour to get things sorted out here. That okay?

That was simultaneously not much time and a lifetime. I agreed and set my phone aside, thinking quickly. One hour until I was in his painfully beautiful presence again. One hour until I got to kiss those soft lips. Damn it, I wanted him there now.

But I also had things to sort out. I needed to talk to Shauna. We needed to hash out our game plan for the band's set at the festival, and I wanted to warn her of Felkyn's imminent arrival rather than being caught.

I dressed quickly in a white band shirt tucked into a black pleated miniskirt over black fishnets. Rather than battling the slow coffee maker, I pulled a can of coke from the mini fridge and headed across the hall. At my knock, Shauna opened the door, holding a steaming mug of black coffee.

"Look at you, bright eyed and dressed up before ten thirty," she appraised, smirking, as she stood aside in the doorway for me to walk in. "Hey, thanks again for your miracle drug. I'm sure going to miss that until we're working together again."

"Well, you can have the rest of my stash if you want," I told her, deciding not to remind her that after today, we weren't working together anymore. I sat on her bed and opened my can of soda. "I probably won't be needing it again for a while. Last night was...sobering."

"Pffft," she guffawed. "Locking yourself out of a hotel room in the middle of the night is *nothing*. Trust me. I've done a ton of stupider shit, and I'm not yet thirty. Shake it off, and enjoy your twenties."

Rather than argue, I took a drink from my soda.

We transitioned into talking about business and the general plan for the day, but my hyped-up brain could barely focus. Everyone else was already en route to the fairgrounds to battle the festival traffic. As the makeup artists, Shauna and I weren't needed until closer to the set, and we preferred to stay out from underfoot. They'd loaded our supplies into the van yesterday, so we were free until mid-afternoon.

I'd assumed I'd need to be in the band staging area by three for the five o'clock set, but Shauna threw a curveball at me and told me they wanted to see me earlier, at two o'clock for a *meeting* with the band and their manager.

We never had meetings. I wondered if I was fired because they'd figured out what Bentley had.

This would have sparked my anxiety into a panic if Felkyn weren't on his way there. He could fix it so I still had a job—though I hated the idea of him pulling strings for me. At the very least, he wouldn't let me be homeless while I figured out my next steps.

While I sat on her bed, my legs bounced uncontrollably and my fingers played with the pull-tab on my soda.

"What's with you, girl?" Shauna asked, cutting through the raucous in my head. "You're not one for pre-show jitters. What's going on up there?"

I tapped out an erratic tinny rhythm on the side of the can while I thought. I hadn't figured out what to say to her, but the minutes were ticking away.

"You know I didn't do anything questionable to get this job, right? Like, you know I didn't have someone important pulling strings for me, right?" I asked after a moment.

"Even if you did, it doesn't matter." She shrugged. "What have I been telling you this whole time? In this business, a leg up is something to be used without guilt or shame. Why?"

"I just...I don't want anyone thinking I'd pull something like that. Or have someone pull something like that."

"Is this because of what Bentley said about you getting your job because of that guy from LV?" She scoffed. "Don't let him get to you, love. *He* got his job because his ex is the drummer's cousin. *I* went to high school with the frontman. And *you* were connected to the opening band. They were already aware you knew your way around a makeup palette. Fuck Bentley."

I nodded but stayed silent. My legs bounced away.

"What's up, Danielle?" she asked, staring at me with a furrowed brow. "Why the sudden need for validation?"

"I called my ex last night," I blurted after a beat.

She jerked her head back, bewildered.

"*Weird* segue," she said, crossing her arms. "Explain. Because of the song? What, was he a dirtbag that thought you couldn't do anything without help?"

"No," I said, almost smirking. *The opposite. The exact opposite.*

"What, then?"

"The song is about me, Shauna. I'm *that* Danielle."

Her expressions alternated through a number of emotions, from disbelief to perplexity, to awe and then to wonder. Nowhere in that myriad of emotions were anger or suspicion, though, so I felt emboldened to dive into the whole watered-down story we'd given the police. She'd heard of the ordeal with Alexis's death, my disappearance, the tragedies back home, but she'd never connected it to *me*, of course. And Felkyn'd been so careful keeping the connections between my case and theirs separate.

"I left them—and broke things off with Felkyn—after the guitarist died and the band fell apart. Because I needed to figure stuff out on my own. Everything was just...so much. And I didn't know if I loved him or if I was just trauma bonded to him...Until last night I still wasn't sure."

"Wait...did I witness rock history last night?" Shauna said. Her jaw was perpetually slack now, but the corners of her mouth tipped up into a giddy smile. "An epic love rekindled with a siren's song?"

"Hah," I chuckled softly, but humorlessly. "I don't know about that. But...I called him. We talked, and it was so easy. I...I miss him."

"And when is the reunion?"

"Soon. Real soon," I said, trying to hide my smirk. I didn't know how much time had passed, but really, it was any minute now. "He's coming to Groezrock."

"He is!?"

"Yeah. It's good timing, too, I guess." I shrugged, tapping my empty can again. "With work ending and all that. I really didn't want to go back to Ireland."

Her smile waned, and she looked at me with cautious wariness.

"Danielle, hun, you didn't call him just because you didn't want to return to Ireland, did you?"

"No. Not really," I protested, honestly. "Not consciously at least..."

She let out a long sigh and rubbed her temples. "I think I should tell you something I've been asked to keep to myself until this afternoon. The reason for the earlier meeting time—"

Before she finished her sentence, my spine stiffened and my eyes shot to the door. I'd heard a faint knocking—like someone knocking on a door across the hall. I patted the pocket of my skirt, but it was empty: I'd left the phone in my room. That gentleman was knocking on the room I said was mine rather than shifting inside it. But how long had he been knocking?

"Afraid I'll just have to be surprised at the meeting," I said, speaking softly, hoping his super hearing didn't pick up on my voice. I stood up from the bed and dumped my can into the trash can. "He's in the hall."

"He is?" She squeaked, both in disbelief and giddy excitement. "Jeez, that was fast."

"Yeah, he was, uh, already in town for Groezrock," I murmured, carefully creeping to the door. I turned back to Shauna and pointed at her sternly and whispered, "*Don't* spy. I promise I'll introduce you later."

She begrudgingly nodded and stayed where she was, crossing her arms.

I peered through the door's peephole, and sure enough, there he was: tall, blond, and magnificent. His back was to the door, and he was glancing down at his phone—probably texting me because I wasn't answering. His hair was the same shoulder-length layered texture, but the blue and purple streaks in his hair were gone.

He turned when I opened the door and stepped into the hall, his eyes roving from my face to my toes, then returning to my face as a grin spread across his. I kept the suspense going just long enough for me to close the door behind me, then I leapt at him.

I threw my arms around his neck, and he lifted me easily against him. I wrapped my legs tightly around his middle, practically climbing him like a tree, and his chest rumbled with laughter against mine. At first, I hugged him, burying my face in his neck, but then I pulled back so I could look at his beautiful, tan face. His golden eyes stared adoringly into mine. Before him, and after, no one had looked at me like that. He brushed his knuckles gently across my jawline, then cupped the back of my head, guiding my face down to his until our lips touched and the world around us melted away.

I wanted to live in that kiss forever. It was sweet and satisfying in ways I never thought a kiss could be, and while it was hungry and full of need, it wasn't impatient. We had all the time in the world to explore each other, and somehow in this reunion kiss, I felt every moment that forever promised in my core.

"Hi, my beautiful dove," he murmured softly when our lips parted moments later. His hand toyed idly through the layers of my hair.

I couldn't explain the reason behind the shiver that thrilled through me when he called me by that pet name. Why did I like it? Was it just because it wasn't something creepy like baby or cringy like sweetheart? I didn't know, but it excited me.

"I've missed you so much," I said softly, running my hands through his soft surfer waves. "It's been a hard, *dumb* time without you."

"And I want to hear all about it," he said, moving his hand from my hair, down my back, then to my thigh, giving it a loving squeeze. "I'm all yours. Whatever you want to do."

Reluctantly, I unhooked my ankles and slid down until my feet were back on the floor. I swiped my keycard in the door and ushered him into my room.

"I figured you'd bring waffles," I joked, smirking at his empty hands.

Back when he rescued me from my cell, he'd asked what I'd wanted to eat first, and my first response had been waffles. Felkyn, a sap even then, had made sure I had authentic Belgian waffles when I woke the next morning.

"If I had, we wouldn't have had that awesome, steamy hug in the hallway," he retorted, grinning. His hands gently gripped the sides of my skirt, pulling my hips against his. "Besides, we're in Belgium, my doveling. Waffle options abound."

As if in on the conversation, my stomach rumbled, vibrating between us. I was noticeably hungry for the first time in I didn't know how long. Was it for real food or for him, though? I couldn't say.

"Take me to breakfast?" I asked, gripping his naturally tanned arms and staring up at him with big eyes.

"I'd love to." He purred, running a thumb over my lips.

We left the hotel and within blocks found a waffle bar with an outdoor patio that, on a Friday in the late morning, wasn't crazy busy.

While I'd been in this town in Belgium for more than a week, this was my first time indulging in authentic waffles. My appetite was fickle and most of the time nonexistent. I'd been surviving on the barest, cheapest store-bought basics because nothing ever sounded good. But this morning, I was as ravenous as when I was first rescued.

I ordered two thick, crispy waffles, one loaded with chocolate sauce and strawberries, the other Nutella and honey, and we carried the plate outside to the patio. He took a seat, but when I put my plate down and started to sit in my own chair, he grabbed my hand.

"Oh no you don't," he said firmly. He pulled my plate toward him and sat me on his lap, facing away from him. He wrapped his arms tightly around my waist, holding me to him.

"Uh, people can see," I chided him softly when his hair brushed against the back of my neck. I protested, but my stomach was quivering with butterflies.

"Relax, I'm not going to do anything untoward in public." He reached around me and picked up my fork, placing it in my hand. Then he kissed my shoulder. "I'm just making up for ten months of touches however I can. Now eat."

I dug in, trying not to appear as ravenous as I was, but it was difficult. While I ate, we filled each other in on the lighter events of the past year. I told him about meeting Aoife and Declan and the cities I'd traveled to since, and he described the dissolution of the band, his regrets in bugging Riley to the point that he forced radio silence, and his starting to teach music lessons to innocently find his prey.

His hands roamed the whole time, finding new places to innocently caress—from the inside of my arm to my shoulder to my hip—making me tingle all over. Between topics we'd kiss innocently, but he'd lick the sweetness from my lips in such an innocently sensual way that it chased whatever words were on my lips away and sent heat to my ears and between my legs.

"I've been wondering for a while what your style was," he mused after I'd finished eating and turned on his lap so I was angled across it rather than facing away from him. His hand was on my knee, but he idly grazed his fingertips higher. "Whether you were simply a jeans and T-shirt girl, or if you wore sundresses or skirts." His hand stopped mid-thigh, and he rested it there, his thumb caressing my inner thigh, just below the hem of my black skirt.

"I'm still figuring out my style," I told him honestly, shrugging. "I don't shop much because I've been making my funds last. So usually it's jeans and tees or hoodies stolen from you guys. But I have a few token outfits for shows, leaning into the emo scene."

"Ah yes, the fishnets. I *definitely like*," he murmured, appreciatively, gently tugging on my tights. "We could go shopping if you want. We can pretend we're in a cliché try-on montage in a movie."

"Maybe, but not today," I said with a laugh at the image. "I've got to be at the fairgrounds by two. But we can walk for a bit if you want."

I imagined, with all his touches and caresses, that walking wasn't exactly what he had in mind. And while I wanted to kiss and stroke him just as much in return, I was scared to start something before the show because we wouldn't want to stop.

His face didn't betray any disappointment or distaste toward my suggestion of a walk, though. We cleared the table and headed on our way.

It amazed me just how *easy* it was to talk to him about anything, as if we hadn't spent almost a year apart and as if we'd known each other for years rather than a handful of weeks before our break. While we walked, our conversation traveled across many subjects, from admiring Declan's band's sound, to appreciating the band I worked for and their aesthetic, to wondering how Riley was doing.

I didn't tell him yet about the Flynns and the struggle of living with them. I wanted to save the topic for later: after the show and after we had some peace.

In an empty courtyard area, we paused and leaned against a wide tree. We stood in contented silence, with my hand in his. His hip rested against mine while he turned sideways, leaning his arm against the tree, above my head. I cupped his jaw with my hand and pulled his face down, melting once his lips met mine.

He deepened the kiss and pressed us both into the wide surface of the tree. His tongue flicked against my lips, and I parted them to let him in. His hands twitched at my hips, as if he couldn't decide whether to move his hands up my sides or down to my ass. Finally, they traveled upward, to the sides of my breasts. His thumbs rubbed the fabric of my shirt roughly, just over my nipples. *Fuck*, even through my bra and shirt, that was exhilarating.

"We're still in public, dear," I murmured teasingly at him, parting our lips just long enough to chide him.

"I know, I know," he mumbled, moving his thumbs back and forth again over my breasts. I groaned and my knees almost buckled. "Don't worry. Until we're alone together, I'll remain PG13."

Until we're alone. The words repeated in my head, and a shiver thrummed through me, melding arousal with that anticipatory fear. I pushed gently on his shoulders, breaking our lips apart so I could look up at him.

"You...you know I'm a virgin, right?" I said, keeping my voice soft, even though no one else was around. "I mean, I *hope* it isn't super obvious that I don't know what I'm doing. But...can you tell I'm a virgin?"

"Can I tell? Like is there a sixth sense in Lapsi that's driven crazy by the smell of virgins?" he asked with a smirk. I'd have been horrified at his words, but I could hear the teasing buried in his tone. He lowered his hands to the narrowest part of my waist and nipped at my collarbone with a growl. "That the thought of ravaging your maidenhood sends me absolutely *feral*?"

"Doesn't it?" My words came out in a gasp because of his love-bite. *Wasn't that just a typical male thought: some seedy satisfaction in being the first?*

"No more than just ravaging you in general," he mused, moving his lips to my throat, and I groaned. He pulled back and looked into my eyes. He brushed my shorter layers off my face and continued in a more sober tone. "It doesn't matter, Danielle. And I'm not in a hurry. We can go as slow as you want, and we'll take that step only when you're ready."

"We don't—We don't have to go slow. And I'm not saying this because I'm like *waiting* or because it matters," I said, my words coming faster and more rambling. I huffed, frustrated. "It's not like I've been saving myself or anything, I just...no one even glanced my way before you."

"I doubt that," he mumbled under his breath, but I ignored it and plowed on.

"We didn't have that much time together before...and there's been no one in between..." I trailed off and took a deep breath to collect myself. "I'm just trying to say...I don't necessarily want to wait, but I do want you to be gentle?" I ended on a question because I realized too late how lame I sounded.

He sighed, but not out of impatience. He brushed my jaw with his knuckles, then cupped his hand beneath my chin and gently angled my face to look up at him.

"Let me be clear, Danielle. By the time I am about to fuck you for the first time—and every time after that—I will have you so aroused, and so ready, that you won't *need* me to be gentle or patient. And you won't *want* me to be either of those things. But I will be. I promise."

The surge of arousal that thrummed through my core at his words was more intense than anything his hands had done so far, and my knees nearly gave out. He grabbed my waist to keep me upright and, laughing softly against my lips, kissed me, long and deep.

My phone alarm went off a moment later, signaling it was time to get to the fairgrounds to prepare for the band's set and have that super vague, probably horrible meeting. I should've been worried about the meeting, since it probably meant my contract wouldn't be renewed, but the promise that he'd be waiting for me, whatever the news, and that we'd spend the rest of the festival enjoying the shows and each other, kept me from worrying about anything.

He hooked an arm around my knees and lifted me into his arms. With one more hungry peck at my lips, he shifted us away to an area of the fairgrounds I'd pointed out to him on the map earlier.

CHAPTER 12

FELKYN

I was on cloud nine.

I never thought I'd say something so corny, but I was. Danielle wasn't holding me at a distance like in the final weeks of her stay with us last year, and I couldn't get enough of it. The taste of her lips, the way her hand fit into mine, and her body against mine. How had I gone thousands of years without knowing how this felt? Without knowing her?

I didn't delude myself in thinking I *couldn't* have loved anyone—or many—over those millennia like I did Danielle. But I know I *hadn't*. Some had come close: like Florence, back in fifteenth century France, or Gillette in Italy, AD 400, but those had been simmering romances and had all perished when the Lapsi curse wedged between us. I never regretted those loves, but I hadn't missed them when we were apart like I had Danielle.

Those ten months were the longest of my life. Every time I felt like the pain should be fading, it flared again, eviscerating me with loneliness. I'd thought relief would come when I finished the song or when it was released. But through each milestone with the song, missing her never faded.

Then she'd called. And I'd been riding a high ever since.

But there were things she was keeping from me. She hadn't yet told me much about her time in Ireland. She'd said it'd been an awful year, and I think it was more than merely her dealing with her grief on her own. It had to do with the Flynns, and she was holding that back.

I understood why, honestly. Today was about rekindling and feeling out whether we still felt as attached as we had a year ago. She didn't want to tarnish our reunion with anything unpleasant.

About thirty minutes after her meeting started, my phone buzzed with a text.

> Oh my god. Oh my god, oh my god!!!

> Where are you? Come back to where you left me!

I shifted back to the spot immediately, and she leapt at me again, throwing her arms around my neck. My arms went automatically around her too-thin waist, while her lips devoured mine eagerly.

"Good news, I take it," I said, when our lips parted.

She'd been assuming it was a meeting ending her contract, but this reaction didn't fit with her expectations.

"Better than I...I never saw this coming," she said, staring past me, still awed. She released her arms from around my neck, and I lowered her back to the ground. She stepped back and combed her short layers away from her face. "The band—they're going to be doing a show. Not a reality show, a scripted drama series, where the bandmates are characters...playing a band."

"That sounds cool," I said when she paused. I'd watch a show about a band where the actors actually knew how to play the instruments.

"Yeah, it's going to be this dark, *vaguely* supernatural drama about this emo band in L.A…" She lifted her eyes to mine, and they were briming with tears. But she was smiling. "And I…I'm going to work on set. I'll be on the same level as Shauna. Not an assistant, not an internship, and not a glorified brush cleaner…a hired artist."

I had no words immediately. Instead, I wrapped my arms tighter around her hips and lifted her against me. I spun in circles, pecking her lips, her neck, and her collarbone—any skin I could reach, really—with kisses. She arched her back in my arms, throwing her arms in the air and laughing while we spun.

"I am so fucking proud of you," I told her, for what felt like the hundredth time in just twelve hours. "It's the dream, dove. Your dream. You fucking did it."

"It…it starts filming in a few months," she breathed when we stopped spinning. She rested her arms on my shoulders and weaved her fingers wistfully into my hair. "I can't…I can't believe it. Shauna had to keep it secret because everyone wanted to tell me in person. They wanted to do it here because I wasn't based in L.A. like the rest of them, and I've been so adverse to flying across the ocean. But now…"

"You're going to move to L.A.?" I asked, dumbfounded. How had this aligned so perfectly? I'd have gone anywhere she went, but I was already established in L.A., so this…this was just perfect.

"I...fuck, I guess I'll have to?" She gripped her face, exasperated. She combed her hair back and shook her head. "God. There's so much to think about...I just can't wrap my head around it."

I pulled her face to mine and kissed her, holding her there until she melted into me, hoping it quieted her thoughts.

"You know I live in L.A., right?" I reminded her when I broke off the kiss. "It'd be an easy commute...or I can get you your own place, rent-free."

"I don't want my own place," she said immediately. "I...I don't do well alone."

"We don't need to figure it all out tonight. But can we celebrate? I'll buy you—I guess it's lunch, since we did breakfast earlier?"

"I need to get back," she said regretfully. "The set's at five, and we need to start on their makeup. Afterwards, though? Buy me dinner and a drink, then we spend the rest of the night watching awesome bands?"

"Absolutely, dove. Whatever you want. My time is yours now," I told her, kissing her long and slow, while I lowered her back to the ground. *Forever. As long as you'll have me.*

I wandered through the festival while she was working but retreated to somewhere private after a short time. Even after eliminating the colored streaks from my hair, I was still too recognizable as Felkyn from Lonely Vagrants.

I'd anticipated being recognized, and I figured a little bit of publicity was okay. I was just an ex-rocker, seeing bands from my genre perform in the same place, and I wasn't the only one. Plenty of others from famous bands were also trickling through the crowds, but most were in the VIP tents. I signed some autographs and allowed a few photos with fans. But whenever any of them asked questions about the LV breakup or who the song was about, I mesmerred their questions away and extricated myself from the growing crowd.

I'd have to be careful when Danielle and I were out in the crowds together. I had been lazy earlier while walking around Antwerp. But I hadn't been thinking about possible cameras capturing our blissful reunion, and now I regretted it. The last thing we needed was a media circus around us, especially with Jeremy at large and undoubtedly still pissed about everything.

The set ended and Danielle met me off to the side of the staging tent after they'd finished packing their van. After a brief introduction to her boss—and now equal—Shauna, we headed to the food stations for her celebratory dinner of fest-fare and locally brewed beer. After that, it was off to the crowds and the stages.

It was a difficult time, as expected. I tried to enjoy the music and performances as much as I could, but it was hard. My neck was constantly on a swivel, scanning for anyone who might be looking at me. Which, of course, caused people to look my way. I'd mesmer them into looking away and erase my face from their short-term memory. Occasionally, one tried to talk to me, but as soon as I heard, "Hey, aren't you—" I'd mesmer them so impatiently, it was amazing their necks didn't snap from turning so quickly.

It got a little easier once the sun began to set, but by the third performance, I was running lower on patience and power than I liked, which made me low on other things: like focus, and *restraint*.

Danielle looked amazing in her element, jumping with everyone else, dancing side to side when it was a song she didn't necessarily know. Through the sounds of the crowd and the music, I could practically hear the sweat as it rolled down her back, soaking into her T-shirt. Sweat also pasted her hair to her temples, and I wanted to taste it. And *hell*, those fishnets. I couldn't take it anymore.

I pressed up close behind her, snaking an arm around her middle, and with my other, I tilted her head back against my shoulder. My lips caressed the spot just below her ear, licking the salt from her skin.

"My dove, I need a break," I growled into her ear, wishing I could project the terrible thoughts running through my head directly into hers. "I'm a second away from either biting the neck of some poor kid in the mosh pit or fucking you right here, right now."

Her spine went rigid at my words and a shudder vibrated through her. Through all other scents of the crowd, I could distinctly smell the swell of her arousal. My hand tensed, grabbing a handful of her T-shirt. *Easy, man. Easy.*

"*Fuck*, I'm not entirely opposed to the latter, but please take me somewhere at least a little private," she said when she recovered from her shock at my words. She reached behind me and gripped my ass playfully.

I laughed and shifted us out of the crowd. We reappeared behind the staging area, in a kind of alleyway made from rows of vans and buses. Once away, she leaned back against a stack of crates, and I leaned into her, dropping my forehead to her shoulder. I let out a small groan, feeling my shoulders relax for the first time in hours.

"Are you okay?" she asked. "What do you need a break from?"

"I'll be fine in a minute. Just...turning people's heads away has me spent." I lifted my head from her shoulder and leaned back against the crates beside her. "I've been trying to keep people from recognizing me and keeping attention off of you—*us*."

"Oh," she said, bringing her hands to her temples. "I didn't even think about that. Shit. I'm sorry."

"No, it's not your fault," I assured her. "I didn't think about it either until we got here. I forgot we'd need to be careful of the press. Then I thought I could handle it, but, jeez, I'm more recognizable than I thought."

"Heh, yeah, I guess you stand out," she said, smirking at me. She reached up and tugged a strand of my shoulder-length blond hair. "Not a lot of blonds-by-choice in the emo scene these days. Maybe a hat would be a good idea? A beanie to tuck your hair into?"

"Good idea, really," I told her. Why hadn't I thought of such a simple solution? "I'll steal one from a merch booth when we go back out there."

"Or we could just go," she offered, with a shrug.

"No, no, no," I told her, whirling in front of her again. I gripped the sides of her face and lowered my mouth to hers. "I'll be okay. I just...it's taken a lot of my power to keep eyes off us." Her fingers wound through my beltloops, and her thumbs hooked beneath the hem of my shirt, gently caressing the bare skin beneath. My hands roved lower, but stopped at the sides of her breasts. I couldn't make my hands move from that spot. I chuckled and smirked guiltily. "And it's made me horny as hell—and irritable. I need to replenish. But I don't want to leave you, and I don't want to make you watch that."

"Then why not take from me?"

"No," I said, rearing my head back and looking at her reproachfully.

"Mine is more sustaining, isn't it?" She drew her hand up and pointed at herself. "Witch, remember? Not full potency, no, but still better than a normal human, in a pinch. I'm sweet and delicious, aren't I? In more ways than most."

"But it will *hurt* you," I reminded her, not appreciating her humor. With her mind still locked down against any external influence, I couldn't make the experience pleasurable for her. And changing her, if ever we decided to do that, would be excruciating.

"I'm of sound mind and body," she said with a half smile. She ran her hand up my bare arm to my shoulder. "Just take a little from me, it'll be fine. My pain tolerance is higher than most."

"Danielle," I protested softly, even as I leaned my body against hers. I had to make her see. "Any time I feed from you, it's going to hurt you. A mouthful *might* be fine, two will burn, probably. More than that will feel like knives..."

"I can handle it." There was almost a challenge there in her eyes, but not to me: to herself. Was she insistent because she wanted to see exactly what she was in for if she chose to change? Fucking hell. This both thrilled me and horrified me. My resolve faltered under the intensity of her gaze. Her hand cupped the back of my head, and her other hand snaked lower, giving my ass another playful squeeze. "And if you feel so bad about it, you can make it up to me right after."

"Five seconds only. And I promise you all the aftercare."

I sighed in a defeated huff and let her guide my lips to her throat. I wedged my thigh between hers, wrapped one arm firmly around her waist, and cradled her head with my other. Then, satisfied she was supported should she spasm or jerk, I willed my fangs to extend into their razor-sharp points and tore open the tender flesh over her artery.

Fuck, I thought as my lips flattened over the cut and blood spurted across my tongue. I rarely took witch blood, and hers wasn't even pure, but still, the difference between it and human blood was astounding. It was sweeter and headier and delicious. But it was also intoxicating. Already, I felt floaty and even more horny, damn it.

She went rigid when I took my first draw of her blood, which I wasn't used to in my victims. It tethered me to reality and reminded me that I had three more seconds. The muscles in her throat tensed and her hands gripped my shoulders tightly, but she didn't push me away.

Two seconds to go and her nails dug into my shoulders while her body convulsed. *I know, dove, I know...*

One second to go and she inhaled quickly though her nose before a shrill exhale escaped her tight lips and clenched jaw.

And then it was over. I pushed away from her with a gasp, but my arm stayed locked around her waist, supporting her. Her body relaxed and her shoulders slumped forward in her relief.

"That wasn't the *worst* thing," she mumbled with a small laugh, her hand going to her throat, which had already healed thanks to my saliva. "Four out of ten, might recommend."

I laughed, and mildly tipsy—and turned on as hell—off the small amount of magic in her blood, I leaned forward into her and kissed her lips. But after a second, she pulled away from me, grimacing.

Her blood dotted her lips, transferred from mine, and she wiped at it furiously. "Okay...not as hot as it is in books and movies..."

I wiped my lips on the lower hem of my shirt and dropped to my knees in front of her. I gripped the backs of her thighs and rested my forehead against her pelvis, relishing the scent of her while the world tilted slowly back into place. The intoxicating quality of her blood didn't last as long as full-blooded witches and was already wearing off. But I couldn't say the same about my uncomfortably hard erection.

"What are you—"

"Shhhh..." I murmured into the front of her skirt, inching my hands upward, under the hem. "Aftercare, as promised."

I ducked my head under her skirt and nuzzled against her thighs while my hands traveled higher and cupped her ass. Above, she gasped softly while I kissed a short trail up her inner thigh. I paused at the artery where her hip met her thigh, caressing it softly with my tongue. It pulsed against my lips, and it was oh, so tempting to tear into it and drink more from her. Instead, I hooked a fang into the netting of her tights and jerked my head roughly. Impatient, my hands came around to assist and tore the fabric savagely away from the delicious V between her legs. The ripping of fabric was almost deafening and sent a thrill shuddering through my cock so intense I nearly came.

"Jesus," she gasped above me, her hands fisting in my hair.

"I'm sorry!" I breathed, sobering and rearing my head back and looking up at her. Had I gone too far?

"It's—it's fine," she said breathlessly. Arousal spilled from her, scenting the air decadently. "Just...you're buying me more."

I chuckled and dove back in. I nipped at the exposed flesh of her thigh joint and, pulling the fabric of her panties aside, grazed her slit with my tongue. She gasped again, but a shudder pulsed through her legs, which I took as a sign to keep going. I nudged her left thigh up and guided it to rest over my shoulder to gain better access for my tongue to explore her.

It wasn't long before she was writhing on my face and moaning softly into her hand. She was close, but I couldn't let her finish yet. No, I wanted to see her face when she came.

I sat back on my heels and surged to my feet, lifting her as I did and pressing her back against the van. She let out a small squeak of surprise, but her legs locked around my hips automatically. She was seated right over my hard cock, and she could feel how hard I was, even through my jeans.

"Remember what I said," she said breathlessly. She'd frozen and stared at me now with big, apprehensive eyes.

She was assuming I was about to fuck her, when really I just wanted to see her reach her climax. I cupped the back of her head and caressed her jaw with my thumb.

"Don't worry, doveling. The first time I bury myself deep inside you is not going to be up against a stranger's van, in the dark, at a music festival. This is only about you," I told her in a low growl. As she relaxed, I patted her knee where it pressed against my hip. "Ease up a bit, here. I've got you."

She obeyed, and I slipped my hand between us to the hole I'd made in her tights. I pushed her panties to the side and stroked her warm, pulsing center with my fingers. I caught her eyes with mine, silently asking to proceed. She nodded, and I stuck one finger into her. Her spine arched, but before she could moan, I locked my lips onto hers, muffling the sound, then stuck a second finger inside her. She writhed on my fingers and, god, it was so fucking hot. My cock throbbed harder.

"I don't have a free hand, so you're going to have to cover your own mouth," I told her when I broke our lips apart. I needed to memorize every detail of her face as she came undone, but I also needed her to be quiet since we were still in public.

When she covered her mouth with her hand, I hooked my fingers inside her and circled my thumb around her clit. With barely any pressure against the bundle of nerves, her orgasm hit with a satisfying violence. She clenched hard on my fingers, and her knees squeezed my hips. And then her face angled backward and her eyes rolled to the sky.

Fuuuuuck...

I wasn't even inside her, yet her orgasm was so intense it pulled one out of me. My cock throbbed and ignited with pleasure that radiated down my legs so violently they shuddered.

As smoothly as I could, I withdrew my hand and wrapped my arms tight around her, leaning us both into the van for support. She rested her forehead on my shoulder, warming my chest with her panting breaths.

Forget cloud nine. I was in heaven. And I never wanted to come back down to earth.

CHAPTER 13

DANIELLE

I wish I could say it wasn't my first orgasm, but—judge all you want—it was.

After our super hot, semi-public tussle, we returned to the festival, Felkyn covering his distinctive locks with a black beanie, and we enjoyed two more sets, until I could barely stand on my feet anymore. We shifted back to my hotel room where I collapsed into the seat by the window with a bottle of water, and Felkyn lounged on the bed, fluffing his hair out from being trapped beneath a hat for the past few hours.

"I desperately need a shower." I groaned, pulling at my hair, greasy from a day's worth of grime and sweat.

With another tired groan, I got to my feet and stretched my back, then sauntered playfully in front of the bed.

"You're welcome to join me, if you want," I ventured, feeling suddenly bold while I took off my jewelry on the way to the bathroom. He'd never seen me naked before, and I still had to explain to him why my stomach was simultaneously more and less scarred since he last saw it. But he'd just given me my first orgasm, and I felt no more restraint around him.

The last piece of jewelry I removed was the leather bracelet. Even though the Flynns insisted I always wear it, I didn't like showering with it.

Felkyn hadn't replied to my invitation and remained oddly silent behind me. Frowning, I turned, then leapt backward with a yelp. He was standing directly in front of me, and his eyes were roving all over me, like he was simultaneously perturbed and turned on.

"There you are," he murmured, his eyes darting over my face.

"What?"

"I can finally sense you," he said, his brow furrowing.

"You can?" My hand flew to my temple. Had my tank of a mind finally unlocked? "You can get in my head?"

"No, not like that. I can...feel you," he said, but at my bewildered expression, he continued. "I've fed from you. Last year and then tonight. And that connects us, meaning I should always *feel* when you're near. It's a defense mechanism so old prey can't sneak up on us. But you...I haven't been able to sense you this whole time."

"Just another way I'm different," I mumbled, rolling my eyes. *When will the wonders of my anomalous blood cease*?

"No, but I *can* now. It's because you took this off." He picked up the leather wrap bracelet from the dresser. "What is this?"

"It's something the Flynns make me wear," I said, but immediately regretted my word choice.

"*Make* you wear?" he repeated, his eyes flashing with alarm and anger. "*What is it*? Why do you wear this?"

"It blocks my magic," I said slowly, choosing my words carefully. "So I can't accidentally access my fire magic in my sleep or unconsciously. It's to help control it."

"Weren't they supposed to be *teaching you* to control it? Not sticking a band-aid on it?" he said, looking incredulously at the ceiling.

"Band-aid's a good term for it. They're all about the band-aids," I muttered, stepping over to the bed and taking a seat with a sigh. "Turns out they aren't as competent in the teaching department as they led me to believe."

His eyes narrowed, and he joined me on the bed. I launched into the full, harrowing story of my early weeks with the Flynns and how the welcoming arms of distant family turned out to be just another cage—a self-imposed one. How they couldn't teach me because my gift was too rare, and how, because of my nightmares, they feared I'd activate it in my sleep. I told him about the sleeping pills to cure the nightmares, the drugged fog that lingered afterward, and them enforcing the bracelet rule. And I explained how Caoimhe and Aoife conspired to dig me out of the grave I'd made for myself.

"Jesus Christ," he muttered when I finished. He stood up and paced, running his hands down the sides of his face then through his hair. "I never would have left you there if I thought it would be like that. How could I let you stay there?"

"I seem to recall not giving you much of a choice in it," I said, looking at him sharply. "I made the plan. I told you to leave. I said no contact. You didn't *let me* do anything."

"Yes, I did. I let you go, even though it broke my heart to do it. I did it because I trusted you to call me if you needed me!"

"And I nearly did so many times. You have no idea how close I got. But I couldn't. I couldn't admit to you that I made a mistake in leaving. I made my bed, and I had to lie in it. But it doesn't matter—"

"You didn't have to lie in it, though! You didn't want to call me, fine. We left you with cash reserves to get yourself out. Or what about Riley? Either of us would have been there immediately."

"Yes, sure," I scoffed. I took on a childish, mocking tone. "Let me call my big bad supernatural buddies because this middle-aged couple was *mean* to me."

"For fuck's sake, Danielle, they were worse than *mean* to you," he snapped, rounding on me. "They drugged you. They locked you in and isolated you. They shackled you with a control collar. How was that less than what the Agathati were going to do? And yet you don't make excuses for them!"

"The difference is that I *chose* to be there. At first it was denial. Then it was apathy. A lot of the time, I wasn't strong enough to hold it all together *and* argue with them. So I waited until I could crawl out."

"You didn't have to crawl out. You could have asked for help! Jesus. I need to know I can trust you to call me for help when you're in trouble. I'll always come for you."

"If I get myself into trouble, I'm going to try and get myself out of it. You like that about me, or did I misinterpret your damn song?" I shook my head stubbornly. "But I fucked up this time. I sagged beneath the weight of everything. They didn't know the extent of my trauma, or my history, and they didn't know because I didn't tell them. It wasn't entirely their fault."

"Not entirely their fault?" he asked, his voice rising in anger with each word. "They *drugged* you!"

"They didn't *force* the pills down my fucking throat!" I yelled, losing my temper at last but not necessarily at him—at myself. "I took them willingly. Every time. Willingly. I knew what they did, and I took them!" I pinned my hands beneath my legs, so he wouldn't see them shaking. Tears pooled in my eyes. "I just wanted—for a little while—to not exist in a world where I had no family, where I had nothing. And I...I liked the feeling too much. I *hid* in that darkness."

His eyes softened, and he walked back to me. He knelt in front of my knees and rested his hands on the tops of my thighs. Before he could say anything, I continued, shakily.

"They were a crutch. One I willingly leaned on, even though I knew I shouldn't. They were numbing, and I was in so much pain." A tear spilled from each eye, and I swiped at them, frustrated. "But I snapped out of it. I weaned myself off them on my own. But I was still fucking depressed and I couldn't *move* beneath the weight."

I took a shaky breath, which hissed through my clenched teeth. "I was broken into a million little pieces. I broke myself even more by going off alone. I realized that too late. But you don't get to bitch me out for how I eventually fit everything back together."

"I wasn't—"

I cut him off with an incredulous scoff.

"You were a heartbeat away from switching into classic victim-blaming shit. 'You should have left,' 'you let them drug you,' 'you let them put the bracelet on you,' 'you should have fought them.'" I listed them off with a mocking tone. "And you're not wrong. Yes, I let them do these things. Yes, I should have called you. But I didn't. And I'm *fine*."

I spat the last word and pushed his arms off my legs. I stood and stepped around him. I wanted to storm off and slam the door, but I still felt like I had more to clarify. I turned back to him, crossing my arms.

Felkyn rocked back onto his heels, then stood and crossed his arms. His mouth was a hard, flat line, but his eyes weren't angry anymore, just guarded.

"I resent them, but I don't entirely blame them. They're scared little bullies, but they're not villains," I explained finally. "They were ill equipped to teach me, and rather than finding outside help, they just tried to suppress me—to bury me. With drugs. With isolation. With a control collar. But they really didn't need to.

"They offered sleeping pills: a band-aid. Maybe if I'd told them *why* I had such night terrors or told them that I had depression, they wouldn't have done so. But they didn't *know*."

I leaned back against the dresser and gnawed on a thumbnail for a moment before continuing. "They imposed these rules that made it feel like a jail. Which didn't matter, because I didn't *want* to go anywhere anyway. My own heartache, guilt, and regret were what buried me." Tears brimmed in my eyes again, and I sniffed roughly, fighting back the deluge of cry-snot forming in my nose. "But help came. Caoimhe nagged me and pestered me into going for runs and made me get our weekly candy stash. Aoife and Declan pulled me out even further and took me abroad. They all undid the cord around my ankle holding me under. They made it so I could tread water again. I didn't call *you*, but help came in other ways."

He moved toward me, reaching for my hands, but I stepped back, out of his reach. My hand fell on the stupid leather bracelet on the dresser, and I picked it up, twisting it in my hands.

It was an oddly beautiful industrial cuff bracelet made of black leather, with a thick silver chain stitched to it. The silver chain held the enchantment that suppressed my magic and apparently hid me from Lapsi—or was it just Felkyn? I had so many questions about that, but the main one was *why*?

"They suggested I wear the bracelet, and I didn't fight them on it because I thought 'All right, if it'll help y'all sleep at night.'" I shrugged, pulling it taut between my hands. "It suppresses a gift I'm not using. So what? My goals never involved magic, and they didn't suddenly change when I discovered I had any. So I wear something to make it impossible for me to use magic? Fine. It *didn't matter*.

"And maybe I still wear it because I'm marginally afraid I *will* just ignite someday. I'm still broken. Still a mess. I still don't know what I'm doing or how everything works. So, you know, *maybe*."

I glared at the silly thing and concentrated all my resentment into it. "But I won't wear it anymore. Because it hides me from you, and it makes no sense for them to do that. I'll bitch them out for it when I see them next. Or maybe I won't, because it doesn't matter now. We're together, despite their meddling, and I'm not under their thumb anymore."

The leather ignited with a pop, and I held it in my palm, watching it curl and burn. My gaze flicked up to Felkyn for a second. His eyes were still guarded, but he couldn't hide his awe. I was sure he'd had the same thought: I shouldn't be able to burn it if it was meant to suppress me.

Soon, all that was left was the silver chain, which glowed a molten red in my hand. I curled my fingers around it and dropped my hands to my sides.

"And I'm not under *your* thumb, either," I said boldly, looking up at him.

The spark of awe disappeared, and so did the guardedness. Instead, he looked like I'd slapped him. And stabbed him. And kicked his dog.

"You're here because I *want* you here. I didn't call you last night because I needed your help. I didn't need saving—if you recall I *was* in trouble but said *no* to you saving me." I rubbed my temple and brow roughly with my free hand. "Take the shining armor off, step off the horse, and don't make me regret calling you."

From the stricken look in his now-huge golden eyes and the way his mouth still hung open, I knew I'd won. I didn't get any cruel satisfaction out of winning, just a tired relief that it was over. He backed up and sat on the bed, dropping his hands uselessly into his lap.

I sat next to him and took off my shoes. When they dropped to the ground with a thud, Felkyn wrapped an arm hesitantly around my shoulder and drew me sideways into him. I leaned my head on his shoulder, and he kissed the side of my head.

"Fuuuuuck," he murmured softly, exasperated. "I never wanted to be on the receiving end of your fire. It never looked fun, and now I can confirm: it doesn't feel good at all. Two out of ten. Definitely don't recommend."

The callback to my earlier joke tickled my heartstrings a bit, but not enough to bring even a shadow of a smile to my lips.

"I'm gonna shower," I told him. He dropped his arm from my shoulders as I sat up straight.

"I'll be here," he said, thankfully picking up on the fact that his invitation from earlier was rescinded. I needed time alone.

CHAPTER 14

DANIELLE

When I left the bathroom, towel wrapped tightly around me, Felkyn was seated on the bed—not quite where I'd left him but close. He'd swapped his jeans and V-neck for a pair of sweats and a white tank, which amused me, because he hadn't come with a bag earlier. I stepped farther into the room and caught sight of a black suitcase that hadn't been there before.

Awful presumptuous assuming you're staying with *me*, I mused, but I kept my face vacant while I crossed the room. I was gauging his energy, but he was doing the same to me.

"I figured you'd be off murdering my would-be captors in a vigilante rage," I teased him carefully. I stepped in front of him, and his knees brushed my bare ones. I ran a hand through his hair.

He let out a huff that was half-sigh, half-snicker. "I wouldn't do that," he said deadpan. He was anything but a killer. The only life he'd ever taken had been accidental—and had led to his being made into a Lapsus by witches. He leaned into my hand like a cat as I brushed it through his hair. "Besides. You said they had a daughter who lives with them. I couldn't justify traumatizing her with her parents' murder."

"Yeah, they're good with her. It's just me they dislike."

I dropped my hand from his head and started to take a step back, but he grabbed my hands before I could. He lowered his forehead to them, kissed them, and looked back up at me.

"I'm sorry for getting angry," he said, staring into my eyes. "It wasn't directed at you. Just them. I'm so sorry it wasn't what you wanted. You needed support, and all you got was resentment and loneliness. I know a little about that..."

"Yeah, did I get a glimpse into the Lapsi way?" I asked with a small chuckle. "Did I pass?"

He reached out and grabbed the towel at either side of my hips. Even though he didn't try to pull it off me and only used it to pull me closer to him, I stiffened. I clutched my arms tightly to my chest and drew my elbows in to keep the towel firmly in place around me.

"I'm so proud of you, Danielle," he said softly. He slipped his hand between the open seam of the towel-dress, and I tensed, praying he wouldn't touch my stomach. But he merely cupped my hip and brushed my bare skin with his thumb as he continued. "Whatever you had to do, however you got out, whatever help you got, I'm proud of you. I'm always awed by you, but now that I know everything that happened while we were apart, I'm blown away."

"Well, you don't know everything," I admitted, biting my lip. I stepped back so his hand dropped from my hip. I fiddled nervously with the folds of fabric where the towel was secured. "There's one more thing. And it's something I have to show you. But before I do, I need you to understand that *I* did this. It was my choice. Dumb as it might have been, I don't regret it."

"Okay," he said, clearly trying to keep his expression neutral, but he couldn't hide his wariness.

I steeled myself because there was no way to do this without either exposing my top half or my bottom half, so I decided not to choose and just bare everything to him. I had no shame anymore, not with him. I released the towel-dress and held the two ends open out to my sides.

At first his eyes sparked with gleeful surprise, but then he realized what I was trying to show him. His expression changed between a few different emotions: from confusion to denial, to wonder and mild horror.

"You—but Andre said they wouldn't heal. They couldn't heal—"

I stood still as he reached out, running the pads of his fingers over the white ridges that crisscrossed my abdomen. A patchwork of burn scars covered my whole stomach, where for a time angry red slashes had spelled the words "sloppy seconds." It'd been a cruel taunt by the Kryrie, carved into my skin with dark magic that prevented the wounds from healing without scarring.

"I'd always planned to burn them away," I explained. I was prepared for his reproach, but I had to say my piece first. "I couldn't stand the reminder every time I looked in the mirror or the thought of anyone else seeing them. It's bad enough I have all the other scars, and *these*." I brushed a finger over the puckered pink scar on the side of one of my breasts from a cigarette, courtesy of Karson. I had a matching one on my other side. "But the words...I needed them gone."

"Jesus," he blurted, horrified. He pressed his palm flat against my stomach, and his other clutched my hip. I knew he was horrified, but his touch on my stomach and hip vibrated warmth through me, which was distracting. "That's insane."

132

"Aoife's a healer," I assured him quickly. "She was there and worked her magic on the aftermath. She's good at what she does, and it didn't take long to heal."

It was a half-lie. Aoife *was* great at her craft, but it hadn't been an easy healing process. I'd been bandaged for weeks, and the pain sizzled from the healing wound for days. I still suspected Aoife purposely made the process less pleasant to punish me for my rashness. It didn't matter though: I never regretted it.

"I...I can't decide whether I'm horrified, awed, or turned on," he admitted, still staring at the rippling, unsightly flesh of my stomach with a mix of all of these emotions.

"That's exactly what Aoife kept saying, too," I quipped, smirking.

He pulled me closer to him, until I was seated across his lap. One hand rested on my hip, and the other supported my shoulders as he nuzzled into my neck, then kissed a line from my shoulder to my chest.

"You really are a phoenix, aren't you?" he murmured, bringing his face to mine. "Risen from the ashes, born anew."

I scoffed and rolled my eyes. "That just sounds like heavy flattery."

I moved to swat his shoulder but shrieked and nearly fell out of his arms when he squeezed the back of my knee. He caught me and repositioned me on his lap, nibbling playfully at my neck, while his hand slid smoothly up my inner thigh.

I let out what I thought would be a mewling, sensual keen, but it turned into an involuntary yawn.

"Fuck, I'm sorry. I'm so tired..." I sagged against him, leaning my head onto his shoulder.

"You can sleep, then. Don't stay up for me." He ran a soothing hand up my back.

I nodded and rolled lazily off his lap. While he hung my discarded towel in the bathroom, I threw on an oversized T-shirt and a pair of boy shorts and climbed onto the bed.

"I'm tired to the bone, but I don't know if I'm going to fall asleep easy," I admitted to him as I nestled in among the pillows. "I'm still pretty wired but, like, don't want to move."

"Maybe I can help you unwind enough to fall asleep," he said, squeezing my knee. "A massage maybe? Is it your legs or your back?"

"Everywhere." I let out a groan as I lengthened into a full-body stretch. "I'd be an absolute idiot to pass up a massage from a gorgeous man."

Everything complained when I sat back up and leaned into him. I captured his lips with mine, and he gripped fistfuls of my shirt at my hips.

"Let's get this back off though," he purred against my lips and lifted the shirt over my head so I was exposed again in just a pair of tiny shorts. "Lie on your stomach, dove."

I obeyed and folded my arms beneath the pillows. He worked his thumbs gently but pointedly into the muscles of my calves, which were sore and angry from hours of jumping on my toes. But he worked his way up my legs, focusing on each muscle group and giving everything more attention than they'd ever gotten before.

He didn't massage my ass with as much candor because I couldn't stop giggling when he tried, but before moving to my torso, he walked his fingers down between my legs where wetness was already seeping into the fabric of the shorts. Then he swept his hand slowly back up. Even over the fabric, the touch drew a mewling whimper from me and sent electricity through my center.

His thumbs pressed between my shoulder blades and a blissful groan rose to my lips. He laughed at the sound and kissed my shoulder before continuing his thorough massage of my back.

After a few minutes, as the tension left my upper body, he leaned down again and planted more kisses up and down my back. He kissed my neck, my shoulder blades, my arms, and my sides. His lips had the opposite effect from his massage and sent heat through me, pooling between my legs.

Sleep was quickly becoming the last thing on my mind. I wiggled beneath him until he adjusted his legs and I could roll onto my back.

"This stopped being relaxing, but I'm not complaining." I raked my hands through his hair.

"Allow me to continue, then."

He attacked my front with the same sensual attention as he had my back: kissing my throat down to my pectorals. His lips clamped around a nipple, and I half-gasped, half-squealed. My back arched, pushing my hips up against his.

He chuckled and kissed lower, making a trail down my stomach.

"Dove, I could listen to you make that sound forever."

His fingers hooked around the waistband of my shorts, and he paused, lifting his head only enough to look at me.

Is he asking for consent? Yes. Fucking yes. I tried to make my nod as obvious as I could, and he laughed again. I gripped the pillow beneath my head as he pulled my shorts down and gently maneuvered them around my ankles.

"Dove, you're magnificent. These legs..." He hooked my leg over his shoulder and caressed the thickest part of my inner thigh with his mouth. "And this ass—" he palmed one of my cheeks and purred against my leg. "—are decadent. And this pussy...my, my, phoenix..." He pressed his lips to my lower ones, and I melted into the sheets. "So wet and warm. Do you burn for me, phoenix?"

He didn't wait for my response—as if I could have given one in that moment—and dove in with his tongue. For the minutes it took him to get me to orgasm, I was a moaning, squirming blob of sizzling sensation, while he licked and suckled on my clit and pumped one—then two fingers into my pussy, curling them inside with expert precision.

The warmth built in my core until it burst, igniting my veins with pleasure. My legs tensed around his head—but what were legs anymore? I threw my head back into the pillow and my back arched—surely making me look like a woman possessed. But I was. Possessed by pleasure that coursed to every nerve ending like electricity. I pressed a pillow to my face in time to muffle the cry that ripped from my lungs.

After I didn't know how long, he released me from the waves of burning current and I collapsed back onto the bed, limp and panting like I'd just run a hundred-meter sprint. He stroked my legs and nipped at my inner thighs as aftershocks rippled through my core.

He gave me a moment to catch my breath before he dove back in.

It was too much, and it was not enough. I could live in this bliss, but I needed a break from this relentless current of fire and pleasure. *No, not a break, just different*, I realized. My curiosity spilled over the edge. I'd had his mouth, and I'd had his fingers inside me. Now I wanted the rest of him.

I lifted my leg and pushed his shoulder with my foot, hard enough to push him away from my sensitive areas. I propped myself on my elbows, and he looked up at me, his mouth open in surprise.

My brain stalled, trapped in those gold eyes. I had no idea what I was going to say. *I think I'm ready*, sounded so *virginal*, even if it was true. This moment called for something flirty or suggestive—neither of which were easy for me.

"Can we even the playing field here? I need you to shed some clothes, too," I said finally after my brain restarted. "And maybe put other parts of you to use."

He closed his mouth and crawled up beside me, pulling me against him.

"You're sure?" he asked, squeezing my hips. "We can wait."

"I'm sure. Only..." A blush spread across my face, and I bit my lip, embarrassed by what I wanted to ask. But his mouth and chin still glistened with my arousal and...while the books I read made this sound hot, I wasn't into that. "Can you, uh, wash your mouth before kissing me?"

He paused for a second, processing the request, but he grinned and nodded. He kissed my shoulder and rolled away and off the bed.

"Whatever you want, I'll do it," he said and disappeared into the bathroom.

While he was gone, I sat up and scooted back against the padded headboard, running my hands through my hair to smooth out the still-damp locks that had been scrunched into the pillows. I tried not to be nervous. I'd had my own Felkyn fantasies when I was feeling particularly lonely. I shouldn't be nervous that one was about to come true, but I was—even while my orgasm-riled brain was still saying *yes, yes, fucking yes!*

He came back into the room wearing only a pair of black boxer briefs, and I tried not to shrink in on myself, self-conscious. He was a thing of pure beauty: lean with a toned chest, arms worthy of a Greek statue, naturally tanned skin, and not a flaw in sight thanks to his Lapsus blood. He'd even wet his hair a little, to fix the crimps in it from wearing a hat earlier, so he looked freshly showered. *Fuck, and he's mine.*

He crawled onto the bed, kissing my leg a few times on his way, until he was beside me. He curled his arms around me and pulled me onto his lap.

"I promised this would be enjoyable for you," he murmured, massaging my jawline with his hand and kissing me, deep and tender. His other hand cupped and kneaded my breast, making my breath catch against his lips. "Just making sure to keep you well stimulated until we begin. Wouldn't want the sensations to fade before I have my way with you."

"Mmmmm, you're really going to ruin me for anyone else, ever, aren't you?" I said, smirking.

I shifted on his lap so I was fully atop him with my knees on either side of him. I would soak his boxers like this, but I didn't care.

"So, I'm not a total prude, just so you know," I said, struggling to think while he took one nipple in his mouth, nibbling at it until it was stiff and tender. "You might be my first—hell, earlier that was probably my first real orgasm—but...I read plenty of spicy romances and kind of know what to expect..."

"You've done your research," he growled against the flesh of my throat. "Is there anything you're sure you *don't* want?"

"No 'taste yourself' in any way, shape, or form," I said automatically, suppressing a shudder. "Your fingers stay out of my mouth, and if you touch my toes, we're over."

He chuckled, but not mockingly. He nodded acceptance and slipped his hand between me and his boxers, rubbing a gentle, barely-there circle around my clit.

"And you?" I said breathily, trying to focus beyond what his finger was doing to me. "Anything you're not into?"

"Exhibitionism," he said after a beat. "No one gets to see my ass or my dick but you. Other than that, whatever you're comfortable with."

"And is there anything special I should know about...fucking a Lapsus?" *Focus, focus, focus, Danielle*, I told myself while pressure built again in my core, thanks to his teasing.

"Like? Like do I have any extra appendages beside my dick?" he asked, amused, as he added just a little more pressure to his circling.

"*Fuck*," I breathed into his neck with a shudder. But I straightened and looked at him, frowning. His teasing while we talked about important things wasn't fair, but two could play at that game. I shifted back on his lap and pulled his hard cock free of his boxers. I took a second to admire it—it was by no means small, but I didn't panic imagining taking it all inside me—then I wrapped a hand around its base.

"Like, can I get pregnant?" I asked, gently running my hand up his shaft.

"No. Not a possibility," he admitted, staring down at my hands. He licked his lips and shook his head to clear it. "Aside from basic lubrication, there's no real...fluid involved in sex. Although there's something I should mention—"

He shuddered and threw his head back unexpectedly when I ran my thumb in a circle over his tip. His whole body shook for a few seconds, and I released his cock in my surprise. He recovered and sat forward again, resting his head on my shoulder and giving my ass an affectionate squeeze.

"I was going to say...Lapsi can...keep going...as long as they want," he said, his voice shaky, but it normalized the longer he talked. "I'm not limited to coming just once, or even just twice. We go until you or I can't stand it anymore."

"Did you just...come just now?" I asked, still a little startled. I'd barely done anything.

"It's been a while," he defended himself, lifting his head from my shoulder and looking at me through half-lidded eyes. He swept a hand through my hair, giving it a playful tug at the back. "I'm a little touch starved, so don't judge me."

I giggled and held up my hands in apology. He grabbed my waist and pulled me closer to his chest again, kissing my neck. His shaft pressed against my clit, and I found myself rubbing along it without realizing it.

"So, uh...how do you want me?" I asked, breathlessly, grabbing the top of the headboard instinctively.

"Well, dove," he purred against my neck. His lips grazed my ear, making me shudder. "You can stay as you are, and I can guide you onto me. Or I can lay you down and plunge myself into you. Really, the question is: how do you want *me*?"

"Forever," I breathed without thinking. He pulled his head back and looked into my eyes with a mix of surprise and regret in his suddenly shiny ones. He knew that by forever, I meant immortality. Regardless if it hurt, I wanted forever, and forever with him.

He kissed a line down my jaw to my chin, then down the center of my throat. His hands gripped my hips and lifted me, guiding me to put my weight back on my knees.

"Hold yourself there for a moment, okay?" he instructed softly. While I obeyed, he grazed one hand up my body until he clasped the back of my neck affectionately. With his other, he gripped his cock, angling it beneath me until it brushed my entrance. My breath hitched and my pulse spiked in anticipation, but I didn't move. "When you're ready, dove, lower yourself onto me. Gentle and slow as you want."

Fuck, I didn't realize instruction would have me weak like this, I thought, shuddering at his words. With him poised at my entrance, I couldn't hide what his words did to me.

Slowly, I relaxed my legs and lowered myself down. I expected pain and gasped at the absence of it as I slid halfway down his cock and paused. We both groaned as one, and he moved his hands and gripped my hips tightly.

"Atta girl," he said in a gasp as I pressed myself the rest of the way down. He continued instructing in a shuddering, halting cadence. "I'm all the way in now—fuck—give yourself a breath to—get used to me here, then start moving. I'll help."

As he spoke, he rocked his hips gently, thrusting inside me just a little more to help me stretch comfortably around him. There still wasn't any pain, just pressure at his girth spreading me. Already I was ready for more. I lifted my hips and worked myself up and down on him, slowly at first, but I picked up the pace as the pleasure built. Our cries matched each others' and we did our best to muffle them with kisses—to lips or various body parts—but for the most part we didn't bother. We were both touch starved, and the bliss building from our joining was overpowering our restraint.

His muscles shuddered and he nearly threw his head back against the headboard again, but instead he growled and wrapped his arms around me, rolling us both until I was beneath him. He pulled out and knelt over me, a golden god with a halo of long hair hanging forward into his eyes.

He grabbed at his boxers and, without bothering to pull them off, tore them from his body, which sent a surprising thrill shuddering through me. *Jeez, do we both have a fabric-tearing kink? We should probably establish some consent rules on this in the future.*

The thoughts flew from my mind when he descended on me again, showering my hips and dripping pussy with affectionate—and aggressive—kisses before angling himself again at my entrance. He lowered to his elbows and buried his cock inside me again. This time he wasn't gentle, and he didn't instruct, but I had zero complaints. The orgasm built, as if we hadn't even paused, and within a few thrusts, my pussy clutched around his dick, and the orgasm exploded outward from my core in pulsing waves.

He thrust one more time and his whole body tensed. He squeezed his eyes shut, clenching his jaw against his orgasmic moan, but it ripped from his lips, sounding like some savage, feral snarl. At the sound, I came again: just a small, rolling orgasm, but he shuddered and planted his lips to my collarbone to avoid crying out again.

"*Fuck*, my phoenix," he whispered, turning his head and nuzzling my neck. "You're worth the wait, one thousand percent."

"You've absolutely ruined me. I will never fuck anyone else," I murmured in a post-orgasm daze. I grabbed a fistful of his hair and pulled him up to look at me. "One more round to wear me out? I'll probably be able to drift right off to sleep after."

"As you wish, dove," he said, kissing my collarbone again. He rocked his hips, pressing deeper inside me and making my back arch up off the bed.

JUNE

CHAPTER 15

FELKYN

Afer the three amazing days at Groezrock, we left Belgium for my apartment in L.A. where I showed her my new living space and my teaching studio, and we started settling in to living together.

Filming for the show wouldn't start until the fall, so Danielle didn't have any engagements or anywhere to be. We walked the city and visited the beach often. She watched me surf from the safety of the shore, but no amount of coaxing would get her into the water. I should have known better: the almighty, unforgiving ocean was the summation of all of her biggest fears.

For the first few weeks, I took her to new places to eat or we went shopping for this or that or we stayed in and watched movies. When we were in the apartment, we couldn't keep our hands off each other.

Did I mention I was in heaven?

But we spent time apart when we needed it—which so far wasn't often. I had a few music lessons per day, and one of these appointments doubled as a feeding for me. During these times, Danielle called Aoife or Caoimhe, went for a run, or read. And I left the apartment on my own at times, like when the itch for an early-morning surf struck or the occasional errand.

She was stirring eggs in a skillet when I returned to the apartment with the small box tucked into my jacket pocket and her favorite coffee in hand. She wore a hoodie and a pair of short shorts, and her brown hair was swept up into a haphazard ponytail, giving me perfect access to her neck as I sidled up behind her. I pressed against her and snaked my arms around her waist, nuzzling into the crook of her neck. This kind of moment was my favorite. It was absolute *heaven*.

"Mmmm, morning," she murmured, angling her head back and leaning into me.

I murmured nonsense into her neck and kissed it more aggressively, making her gasp and laugh.

"You're going to make me burn them," she managed to get out, while still laughing.

I gripped her tighter for a second and released her and stepped back.

"Sorry, sorry, you know I don't know how cooking works," I teased, biting my lip while I looked at her nearly bare legs. She gave the skillet another stir and flipped off the burner. "You don't think it's a little weird, eating eggs, dove? Seems a little quasi-cannibalistic, doesn't it?"

"Oh, I'm just practicing for, you know," she shot back with a smirk.

She meant of course for when she eventually was Lapsi. It wasn't a taboo subject, but neither of us were in a hurry to make the transition. We'd agreed to wait at least until she was twenty-one at the end of next month, but she also wanted to get through the first few weeks of working on set because she could only handle one big adjustment at a time.

It was going to be complicated since she'd be in agony for all of it and I would get increasingly drunker on her enchanted blood. We had to be delicate and ready.

She brought the skillet over to the small table I'd gotten after our return from Belgium and spooned her scrambled eggs onto the paper plate beside half a bagel. I knew she'd never complain, but I winced regretfully at the plain fare and the cold bagel—we didn't even have a toaster.

"Oh, you got me coffee? Thank you!" she said when she saw the cup on the table.

"You're welcome." I kissed her cheek and took the hot skillet from her hand.

I carried it to the small sink to clean up while she ate her breakfast. Weeks ago, this hadn't even been a kitchen, and it still could barely be called a kitchenette. This space above the music studio was never meant to be lived in: it was more of an office space with a bathroom. The landlord balked when I said I intended to live there and tried to talk me out of it, but after he gave in, his conscience drove him to install a small shower in the bathroom and a fridge and sink in the main room. I never asked him to do that, but now I was glad he had.

Over the past few weeks, we'd added a small table where she could eat and a sideboard for storage, on which was a microwave, coffee maker, and hotplate. There was no counterspace to speak of, and storage was minimal: we kept the singular pot and pan, paper plates, and plasticware on top of the fridge for lack of better places. She was grateful I'd been able to accommodate this much, but it was a sad sight.

"I think once filming starts, I'll contact the landlord and work out an arrangement to get an official kitchen put in here," I told her when I'd finished cleaning up and took the seat next to her. "Hell, I'll just offer to buy the whole building from him. That way we can expand upward too. Have multiple rooms, multiple spaces for different things..." Her wary side-eye broke my train of thought and I trailed off.

"You...you don't have to do that just for me," she said, shaking her head. She shrugged and took a sip from her coffee. "I'm used to fitting into whatever space there is."

She was used to contorting herself into the spaces people gave her rather than demanding the space she was due. She'd done it her whole life, being the side character in her best friend's life. Then with us Italy and with the Flynns. Even when she had a hotel room to herself, she'd never unpacked. She deserved all the space to stretch out and make hers.

I leaned toward her and kissed her temple for a long moment, trying to communicate all these thoughts into this one kiss.

"And besides, a kitchen isn't really a high priority is it?" she continued when I pulled away. "I mean, I won't always need one..."

"I know, I know," I told her, getting her meaning. I took her hand and held it firmly in both of mine. "But trust me, we *should* expand our space. The togetherness is awesome right now, and I can't get enough of it. But it will become grating. We need our own spaces and to do as much as we can to curb the effects of Cain's curse."

Her smile waned as I spoke, as it often did when I brought it up, and her eyes lowered to our hands on the table's surface. I tried to remind her as often as I could about the drawbacks to her choosing a life with me, so she knew what she was signing up for.

"You want forever with me, and I'm going to try my best to give you as much of that as I can," I told her, kissing her knuckles. "I love you, and that will *never* fade. But we will need breaks eventually."

"And it does reset, right?" She took her hand back from me, but only so she could climb onto my lap and sit sideways across my legs. I slipped my hand beneath her hoodie and brushed her side idly with my fingers. "You promise it's not a one and done thing?"

"It resets," I assured her, resting my head on her shoulder.

"How long does it take to drive us apart? And how long does it take to reset?"

"I've never tested it extensively. As a band, we were together for about five years and were starting to feel it. I can ask Riley once he's talking to me again. But it could be anywhere from a year to three years to reset, maybe? Which sounds long, but with immortality, that's *nothing.*"

Never mind that this year apart from her was the longest, hardest year of your life, I chided myself, *and you didn't even make it the full year. You both tapped out after ten months.*

This past year was different. In fact, it made me certain we'd be able to do this. There was a string between us, connecting our hearts. We could take time apart, but the tension in that string would always send us ricocheting back into each other.

"We'll always snap together again. It's worth it," I murmured without entirely meaning to. I put my head back on her shoulder, and she leaned her head to rest it on top of mine. "That's not to say that you're not...allowed to experiment on these breaks. Flirt. Seduce your prey. Do whatever. I love you, and eternity is vast and malleable..."

"You'd think you'd wait twenty or thirty years before suggesting we try out *others*." She spoke reproachfully, but her gentle tug on my hair communicated that she was teasing me.

I lifted my head and captured her lips with mine. After a moment we pulled apart, and she nestled her head into my shoulder with a sigh.

"Don't worry, my sweet dove, I'll make you so sick of me, you'll be happy to take a break," I joked, kissing her temple.

"I'll just have to figure out what I'm going to do during those breaks. I'm used to being alone and figuring things out, even though I don't like it. I get...low." She shrugged but didn't lift her head from my shoulder.

She got low and depressed, I knew. I'd seen it at times over the past few weeks. The grief crept in and kicked her into low moods, where she didn't want to move or go out. During those times, I was more than happy to lie with her and hold her until she came out of it. And I made sure she ate, even though her appetite disappeared when she got low like that.

I knew how grief worked and reared its ugly head at random times, no matter how much time passed. Every time there was a new groundbreaking technological advancement, like skyscrapers, elevators, and *planes*, millennia-old grief seared my lungs, because my dad would have loved to see those things.

Lapsi get low and physically shut down too. We bury ourselves in a starved stasis for years at a time. Coming back up is gruesome, but it happens to the best and worst of us. I knew she'd go underground in the future, more than once, surely.

"I'll work and keep busy. That'll be easy enough," she continued after we sat quietly for a moment. "And I'll have

Aoife and Caoimhe. And then Libby as she grows up. But...oh, that's going to be hard. Watching Aoife age beyond me. Watching Libby hit milestones that Colt never will—"

She stopped short and buried her face in my shoulder, and I held her tightly.

"I still want it," she continued finally. She lifted her head and locked her big eyes on mine. "I want you. I want your strength, your heart, to be your equal. As much of forever with you as we can get, I'll take it."

As much of forever with you as we can get, I repeated in my head, liking the sound of it.

"You'll have it, dove. You *already* have it." I ran my hands up her arms, cupping her shoulders, then her jaw. "And even if we're on one of those breaks and you get low, you can call me. Even if you don't need me, I hope you'll call me. But you've already proven that you'll come out of it on your own or ask someone to help dig you out. You rise from your ashes, my beautiful phoenix."

She humored me with a smile, but she rolled her eyes and shook her head gently. She did that when I got too sappy, but I couldn't help it. I grinned and dipped one hand into my jacket pocket.

"Which reminds me...I got you something." It wasn't the greatest segue, but I'd nearly forgotten about the small box in my pocket, until I mentioned *phoenix*. I pulled it out and handed it to her, but before she opened it, I pressed my hands around hers firmly. "Yes, this is a ring. There's no hiding it from the size of the box. *But* I'm not some dumbass that proposes after weeks. It's just something I had designed..."

I withdrew my hands from around hers and sat back while she opened it.

Inside was a silver open-style ring that would wrap around her finger. One end was a feather, set with tiny stones in a fiery gradient, and the other end was the plumed head and chest of a bird, inlaid with more tiny gemstones of red and orange.

"A phoenix," she said, awed, staring down at it. Her eyes were misty.

"I wanted you to have something from me that reminds you of how I see you. But I didn't want to compete for wear-time with your pendant," I explained, stroking her arm. The Icarus pendant her friend had given her was still a favorite. "And, you know, bracelets are kind of tainted now."

"I love it," she said, pulling it from the box cushion and fitting it onto her right ring finger. She held it out for us both to see, turning it every angle to catch the light. "God...I really do. It's beautiful."

She looped her hands behind my neck and devoured my lips with hers. I slipped my hands beneath her hoodie and snaked them around behind her, pulling her torso into mine.

JULY

CHAPTER 16

DANIELLE

The gate to the Flynns' yard creaked horribly like always and was a pain to relatch. With all the modernity of the interior of their cozy home, they never once thought to replace the original gate. I finally got it to latch, but as I turned, the rusted bottom of the gate caught my pantleg. Swearing, I stumbled sideways, and my bag slipped from my shoulder.

Before it or I could hit the ground, a pair of hands grabbed my elbows and steadied me back onto my feet.

"Thanks," I grumbled, shouldering my bag again. I turned, expecting Mr. Flynn, but jerked back when I found it was a stranger.

He was an ordinary guy around Mr. Flynn's age, but fitter and better dressed in a collared shirt and slacks. His hair was blond and neatly cropped, and he wore glasses. He didn't glance down at me at all as he released my arms and unlatched the horrid gate I'd just struggled to close.

I stared after him for a second, trying to recall any details of his face, but I came up blank. With a shrug, I hiked the bag higher on my shoulder and turned back to the Flynns' house.

I reached their front door and braced myself for a moment before knocking. I wasn't looking forward to the uncomfortable conversation that was about to happen, but it was past time to have it. I'd put it off while I adjusted to living in California with Felkyn, but they hadn't stopped pestering me about coming back to visit "one last time." I finally caved when they pulled the Caoimhe-card, that I owed her a goodbye. Even though I wasn't leaving *her* behind—just her parents.

I couldn't think of a way to deflect anymore without sounding like I didn't care about Caoimhe, so I'd agreed to return to Bray one more time, and I brought the books that'd been sent to me while I'd been with them. I'd never read more than a few chapters of the first one.

The door opened seconds after I knocked, and Caoimhe barely gave me a chance to cross the threshold before throwing her arms around my middle in a fierce, but small, bear hug. My elbow bumped painfully into the doorframe as she pushed me off balance, and I winced in the same breath as a laugh.

"Hey, kid." I snickered, returning the hug and righting our footing. She released me, and I could take her all in finally. "Wait, hold up."

I put a hand to the crown of her head and moved it level with the floor, to my face. She used to only come to my chin, but now the nearly fourteen-year-old was level with my nose.

"Are you in lifts, or have you grown even more?" I asked her, shaking my head, baffled. She giggled and wiggled her upper body like a goof.

"Girls, how about we close the door, yeah?" Mrs. Flynn barked from the kitchen.

My smile stayed intact with effort, but the humor left my eyes, which I kept focused on Caoimhe's face. She snorted, but since her back was to them, she could roll her eyes when I couldn't. Caoimhe skirted around me so she could close the front door behind me and simultaneously nudged me farther into the room.

Mr. Flynn leaned in the doorway between the kitchen and dining room, holding a mug of coffee and frowning at me.

"Sir," I said as neutrally as I could, with a nod of greeting. In almost a year, I still wasn't sure how I should address him: sir, Mr. Flynn, or Colm.

"She's finishing plating up the sausage rolls, so we might as well sit," he said tonelessly and motioned to the table with his mug.

"I—you didn't have to do a whole special breakfast." I walked across the living room to the dining table. It was set with plates and silverware, a delicious-looking egg casserole, and potatoes. "I was expecting muffins at most."

"Caoimhe insisted. Said it would be an early birthday celebration," Mrs. Flynn explained, stepping out of the kitchen behind her husband.

"But her birthday isn't until September." I shook my head. My mouth was watering just at the sight of the plate of steaming sausage rolls in her hands.

"Not mine, yours, dummy," Caoimhe said, pushing me into the chair she pulled out for me. She dropped a bagged present onto my lap. "Did you forget yours is at the end of this month?"

It wasn't that I'd forgotten it. I'd just been trying not to think about it. It was my twenty-first, yes, but my twentieth had been one of the worst days of my life, so I wasn't exactly looking forward to another one.

"Open, open, open," Caoimhe chanted eagerly, plopping into the seat across from me.

Mrs. Flynn dished food onto Caoimhe's plate while I reached my hand into the giftbag and withdrew a black hard-plastic coffin, with gothic etchings on the closed lid. It was meant to stand on its side and had three open compartments for pencils—or brushes.

"Is this a brush holder?" I asked, grinning and setting the coffin-shaped holder onto the table. The Flynns frowned at it, and I knew it was hinting at a dangerous topic, but it was too damn funny. "A coffin brush holder!"

"Yes! I thought it was too perfect," she exclaimed, bouncing in her seat. "You know, because—"

"Because of that book series, yeah," I interrupted her, brushing a finger over my eyebrow—our secret shut-up signal. I glanced between the Flynns. "It's a silly series because, you know, *vampires* are never portrayed as *Lapsi*, but the plot is good—"

"Yeah, that, and the show you're going to be working on, duh. I thought this would be perfect for your workspace because of the show," Caoimhe clarified, looking at me like I should have caught on to that.

"Uh, the show?" My eyebrows knit together before I could stop them. "It's not...I mean, they said supernatural elements, but I don't think they meant—"

"No, I've been researching it. It's totally vampires. A vampire rock band. Which is hilarious," she said eagerly, probably not even realizing how the rest of the table tensed the more she gushed.

"Hah, yeah, I guess...I just haven't looked that deep into it," I said, my laugh thin and fragile. I scratched at my eyebrow more aggressively, but Caoimhe's brow furrowed in confusion at the repeated gesture. Our eye contact broke because Mrs. Flynn handed me a plate of food. I tucked the brush-holder coffin back into the giftbag and put it on the floor by my chair. "It'll be a total hit at work, and I love it. Thank you."

We were quiet while we ate the delicious breakfast. I picked at most of the things on my plate because my nerves were wound too tight to have much appetite. But I couldn't resist the steaming sweetened coffee or the buttery, savory sausage rolls.

"So if you haven't been looking into the show you'll be working on or preparing for it, what *have* you been doing this whole time?" Mrs. Flynn asked just as I forked a bite of sausage roll into my mouth.

None of your business, I thought at first but let it go. Out of annoyance at her timing, I chewed slowly and took a slow, careful sip of coffee before answering.

"There isn't much for me to prepare for at this point. They're keeping me in the loop, but they're just doing table reads right now. Filming doesn't start until the fall, but I'll be called in a little earlier for the promotional photos and set lighting, et cetera." I took another sip of coffee. "It's complicated, but they don't need me until then."

"So then, what have you been up to?" Mrs. Flynn asked again.

None of your business.

"Exploring the city, getting familiar with it. Furnishing my new place. Just hanging out." I listed with a shrug.

"What about the beach? Are you close to it?" Caoimhe interjected, bouncing in her seat. "Is it like our beach?"

"I'm not super close, no, but close enough. The beach is different...it's *browner*, because of the seaweed. But you know I hate the ocean, so I just admire it from a distance."

"I don't know how you're even able to afford a place in L.A. all alone," Mr. Flynn said, speaking for the first time since we'd sat down. "I was looking into it, and rent in that city is expensive. Your new job can't pay *that* well."

"Yeah, well, I have savings. As you recall, back when I stayed here, I had the means to pay you room and board, but you wouldn't let me. I still have those means." I took a sip from my coffee and set it down. "But it's really not your concern."

"But are you staying alone? Or did you find a roommate? Or—"

"Seriously," I snapped, my hands clenching into fists as I struggled to keep my voice from rising. "I know what you really want to ask me, and my answer will be the same it always is: it's none of your goddamned business."

I glared and crossed my arms over my chest. I made sure the sleeves of my zipper sweatshirt pushed up a little, exposing my wrists. As much as I wanted to enjoy Caoimhe's presence, it was time to end the façade and get to the real point of my being there.

"But, sure, go ahead and ask me anyway," I challenged him when he didn't take the bait immediately. I unfolded my arms and flopped my hands in the air, faking more impatience than I felt. "I know you want to."

"Where is your bracelet?" Mrs. Flynn demanded, practically hissing through her teeth.

I hid my triumph and glanced at her venomously instead. I wished they weren't sitting on either side of me, though: the head-swiveling was going to get taxing.

"I don't wear it anymore," I snapped, placing my hands flat on the table by my plate.

"We had an agreement—" Mr. Flynn started.

"Yeah, well, I figured that kind of went out the window when I stopped living here." I shrugged. "Especially since I decided I wasn't coming back here. You're not in charge of—"

"This wasn't about you staying safe just when you lived with us," Mr. Flynn cut me off.

No, I know it wasn't about that at all, I agreed silently, rolling my eyes and setting my jaw into a tense angle.

"It was about you keeping everyone around you safe, in case you accidentally tapped into your magic when you didn't have control."

"Especially with you not taking the sleeping pills anymore," Mrs. Flynn chimed in, her voice gentler than her husband's. "Your nightmares could cause you to—"

"I told you *so many* times that it doesn't work like that." I brought my hands halfway to my temples in frustration before forcing them back to the table.

"But you don't know that," Mr. Flynn said, using the argument he'd used all year. Too bad I saw through it now. "You've never had any training."

"Because you refused to help me with that," I murmured.

"Do you want to run the risk of encountering the wrong kind of stimulation that will set you off?" he continued, ignoring my remark.

"Please!" I scoffed, crossing my arms again and grinning at him. "I've had nightmares so intense you'd *think* I'd ignite if I could. *And* I've had several mind-blowing orgasms, and if they didn't do it—"

"Enough!" Mr. Flynn slammed his palms down on the table, making us jump. I hadn't meant to blurt that out, but his shocked anger was *satisfying*.

"Caoimhe, go to your room," Mrs. Flynn said while Mr. Flynn and I glared at each other.

I slid my gaze to Caoimhe across the table from me as her expression shifted from shocked amusement to defiance. But as she caught my eye, the defiance waned to wariness. I wasn't sure if she didn't want to leave me alone with her parents or if she was worried I'd storm out and be gone forever.

I could handle myself around her parents, and I had things to say to them that I'd rather she not hear. I nodded and apologized with my eyes, and her shoulders sagged in defeat.

"I'm sorry, that was crass," I said after Caoimhe left the room. The tension in the room was palpable, but I was glad Caoimhe wasn't there anymore. Now we could drop the thin façade that this was a happy family breakfast.

"Are you back with *that guy*?" he demanded, his hands in fists by his plate. "Is that who you're staying with?"

"Hmmmm, I'm going to need you to be more specific," I murmured with a cruel smirk, leaning back in my chair. "According to you, I'm a band slut, which implies I slept with each member of the band, so I'm not sure who you mean by *that guy*."

As his face grew redder, I thanked the stars that my nerves had been wound so tight by tension that it unlocked my savage tongue. I wouldn't be able to hold my own against the two of them if it hadn't.

"See, 'cause one of the bandmembers is gay, so, yeah, there's no sleeping with him," I continued when they didn't have a retort. "His brother, the guitarist, died a year ago, so...nope. And the frontman was a relentless asshat that left me for dead. So...nope. Not fucking him. Ever."

"Danielle—"

"Then there's the bassist. But...no, it *can't* be him." I tapped my chin and tilted my head in mock confusion. "Because he fed from me once, which means he'd be able to sense me as soon as he's within a certain radius of me. And you guys *negated* that and masked me from him with this handy dandy bracelet." I uncrossed my arms and looked down at my bare wrist. "Oh...wait."

I cut my eyes back up to Mr. Flynn, all humor gone from my expression. He didn't look angry anymore, but his mouth was set in a hard line. His eyes narrowed, as if calculating his response.

"Was it ever meant to block my magic?" I asked him, taking a careful sip of the sweetened coffee and savoring it. "If it was, it needed something stronger. I shouldn't have been able to *burn it* off me."

"It *was* meant to block your magic," Mrs. Flynn piped up softly.

"And the other thing was just a little extra pizzazz, then?" I snapped.

"To keep you from going back to him too soon—" she parried.

"How did you even know he fed on me once?"

"An educated guess," Mr. Flynn said, finding his voice at last. "His kind can't help themselves."

I let out a small chuckle and rubbed my eye with my free hand. "I am so sick of your bullshit," I murmured.

"Watch your—"

"No. Fuck off," I snapped, putting my mug down and glaring at him. "I'm not here for a courtesy call or because you guilted me. I'm here to say *what the fuck?*"

"We assumed that because you left him, you wanted him to stay away from you," Mrs. Flynn offered.

"We didn't trust him not to track you down—" Mr. Flynn added, but I cut him off.

"Assume, assume, assume. That's all you guys do rather than trust me," I grumbled, rolling my eyes. "You assumed I was a slutty groupie. You assumed I was bullshitting about having magic. Then, when I proved you wrong, you assumed I was a danger to you and everyone. So you sought to control me. You gave me sleeping pills that doped me and made me docile. You pressured me into a control collar. But I'm done with you thinking you can control me. I'm not yours to fuck around with anymore."

"You're so dramatic," Mrs. Flynn said, waving a hand, but her voice wavered. Rather than sounding arrogant, she sounded like she doubted her own attitude. "You needed the sleep—"

"I needed *help*. I needed compassion and space to grieve." I closed my eyes and took a steadying breath.

"We're sorry, Danielle," Mrs. Flynn said, her voice sounding stronger. My eyes slid to Mr. Flynn to gauge whether he was sorry too—he didn't appear to be—then back to her. "You're right to be mad, but let us make it right."

"No thanks." I shook my head. "I'm good, really. I have a job, a place in sunny L.A." *And I have my soulmate.*

"What if we told you we've found someone who can teach you properly?" Mr. Flynn offered as I pushed my chair back from the table.

I stopped and turned narrowed, skeptical eyes to him. Was that the icy, nondescript man who had been outside? *Odd they didn't ask him to stay.*

"I'd say too little, too late." I shrugged and shook my head. "I don't need training for something I'm never going to use. And, like I said, I need compassion and space to grieve, and a chance to move on. I have those things now. With *him.* Because, guess what, your little bracelet trick doesn't work if *I* call him and tell him where I am."

"You goddamned slut," Mr. Flynn growled, hitting the side of his fist on the table.

"You fucking bully," I snapped back, my voice even. I slapped the end of the table with both hands and pushed my chair back a few inches. "You had no right to keep us apart. It wasn't up to you!"

"Danielle, you have to give this more thought," Mrs. Flynn cut in, holding her hands up harmlessly. "It can't last with him."

"It can, though. It can last literally forever." I was bullshitting of course: I was no stranger to the on-again-off-again caveats in our future, but for the sake of arguing, I could ignore them.

I stood from the table and placed my bag in my vacated chair. I pulled out the stack of old books and placed them on the table. "I figured I'd return these, since they're useless to me."

"You can't throw away your magic to become one of them," Mr. Flynn sputtered, standing up and pressing his knuckles into the tabletop. "Your magic is too important—too rare to just give it up! And for what? To not age and remain a perfectly fuckable toy for a *Lapsus*."

"Too important. Too rare," I parroted, again rolling my eyes. I put Caoimhe's giftbag in my bag and zipped it up. "I thought you wanted to suppress my magic this whole time, or did I misread everything?"

"Until we found you a mentor!" he yelled, throwing his hands in the air. "We had to keep you safe and calm and happy until we figured things out!"

"Well you, uh, missed the mark on the happy part." I snorted. "I finally reached some semblance of happy once I *left*. As I said, I'm not interested."

"You can't choose him." He spoke the words slowly and evenly.

"I am, though." I shouldered my bag. "You won't see me again."

"No," he said firmly, narrowing his eyes and setting his jaw.

"Did we fail you that much?" Mrs. Flynn asked, pulling my focus off her husband. Her voice was soft and hurt. "To make you turn your back on your own kind?"

"How can I turn my back on something that never had mine in the first place?" I asked with an impatient shrug, but my voice had softened at her hurt tone. I took a steadying breath and gripped the chairback while I chose my words carefully. "It's not about hating my blood or my kind. I've met terrible witches who gambled with my life, then there's *you guys*, who are belligerent nags. But I love your daughter like a little sister. I love Aoife and Declan and Libby... And I've met a Lapsus who hated me for no reason, who sold me, poisoned me, and left me for dead. But I don't condemn an entire species because of him."

Mr. Flynn was still stewing to my right, I knew, but I kept my eyes on Mrs. Flynn where she sat. For once, she didn't look at me like I was a feral, hissing cat. She'd been genuinely hurt at the idea of me hating them so much that I denounced all witches.

"What's so wrong about choosing a life of love and a forever where I'm not so fragile?" I continued after neither had a retort. "I know the drawbacks. I'm not naïve. But to me the strength and the love outweigh it all."

My words seemed to be cracking her hard, brittle shell. At last I saw kindness—real kindness—in her expression. There was guilt there too, and a bit of indecision.

I released the chairback and stood up straight.

"You won't see me again, if you don't want to," I told them, walking backward, away from the table.

"I'm not going to let you turn your back on your kind," Mr. Flynn said, stepping forward after me.

"I already said I'm not doing that. But I *am* leaving," I told him through clenched teeth. "And you're not stopping me."

"You're not leaving."

"Colm," Mrs. Flynn said softly, still from the table.

"You're not stopping me," I said again, my hand on the handle of the front door.

I threw the door open and shot through it, but my shoulder collided with the solid chest of a man standing on the threshold. With a yelp, I leapt backward and stumbled into Mr. Flynn's waiting arms.

"Colm! Don't do this!" Mrs. Flynn sounded terrified but still far behind us.

Mr. Flynn pressed a damp cloth over my nose and mouth, and I gasped in shock before I could stop myself. With that one breath, spots dotted the edges of my vision.

Fuck!

I writhed to get away from him, but the other man stood directly in front of me, boxing me in. My vision was half-dark, but I tried kicking out against the stranger while I still had strength.

He easily sidestepped me and jabbed a needle into my neck. My limbs immediately felt heavy.

"Fucking bastards," I managed to spit out as Mr. Flynn took the rag from my nose and mouth. Then the darkness pulled me all the way under.

CHAPTER 17

FELKYN

I didn't bother banging on the door of the cottage and instead kicked it in, shattering the human-made lock with ease. The door smacked against the wall, no doubt denting it, but a dented wall was the least of these assholes' worries.

When Danielle hadn't texted after an hour, I'd thought it weird. But when, after two hours of silence, her phone went straight to voice mail, I jumped into action. The house was warded for bear, much like our old Italian cliffside home—which was flattering, I guess, but overkill—so I couldn't shift closer than a block away and had to sprint the rest of the way.

I barreled into the room and froze, twitching with fury. I'd been ready for an ambush, but the house was empty and dead quiet. It still smelled of breakfast, but the dining table was cleared and all evidence of the meal was gone. I could barely detect Danielle's scent lingering in the room. If she'd been there hours ago, I should still smell her.

The house was still, quiet, and magically stripped of her recent presence. They'd performed the spell in a hurry, though, because I could still smell her there, faintly, as if the trail were weeks old.

Neither of us suspected a thing from the Flynns. I should have been more wary, especially after the stupid bracelet, but I'd let Danielle's confidence placate me. Stupid. Stupid. Stupid!

My lips curled back from my teeth in a silent snarl, and I threw a metal lamp across the room where it busted through their closet door, practically shearing it in half. I shifted to the other side of the dining room and hefted the heavy dining table onto its side, sending plates shattering and cutlery flying.

But I stopped myself from continuing my path of destruction and stood, collecting myself. Where the fuck did they take her?

More of Danielle's scent wafted toward me, stopping me in my angry tracks. Still twitching with anger, I crossed the room to its source and knelt by the broken closet door.

Inside was the teal backpack she'd brought there, which was originally Colin's. The books she'd piled into it were gone, and instead there was a sparkly giftbag. Her phone was still tucked into the front pouch. They'd left her things there and masked their scent, as if she would be back. What were they planning?

A floorboard creaked near the front door, and my head shot up.

The girl retreated back with a yelp and tried to turn and run, but I closed the distance between us and grabbed her arm. A sharp pain shot through my forearm as I yanked her inside with me, but the silver knife and her phone clattered to the floor between us.

The Flynns' daughter, surely, I thought, based on the knife. She beat her fists against my chest as I clasped my hands around her neck and squeezed.

I hadn't been this angry in millennia. Not even when Jeremy made me watch as he poisoned Danielle. That'd been *close*, but this felt nearer to the rage I'd flown into when my father and brother died. I'd destroyed my father's workshop and accidentally trapped a child in the burning rubble. That'd been an accident, but was I angry enough to kill a child on purpose?

No. I couldn't. I slowly relaxed my fingers on her throat.

This had to be the sister-figure Danielle spoke highly of. Even if I could set my conscience aside for the moment and kill her, Danielle would never forgive me. But I couldn't just let the kid go.

"*Where is she?*" I demanded in a snarl, grabbing her shoulders and forcing her back against the wall—being careful her head didn't smack the wall. Her mouth still hung slack in shock, and when she didn't respond for a moment, I shook her again. "Where's Danielle? What did you assholes do with her?"

She found her voice finally. "What do you mean *where*? She left!" She still sounded afraid, but her voice held notes of indignation and *hurt*. "And she didn't say goodbye." Caoimhe stamped her foot, reminding me again that she was only a kid.

"She didn't say goodbye because she didn't willingly leave." I released one shoulder so I could pull Danielle's phone from my pocket. I held it up in front of her face. "If she left, why is her phone still here?" I turned her, so she could see Danielle's things in the closet. "And her bag—"

"And the present I gave her." Her eyes were big before, but now they were huge. "Why would she leave those?"

"She didn't," I repeated through clenched teeth. "Your parents took her."

"They wouldn't—" she started indignantly, but the words stuck in her throat. She shook her head again and looked at me fearfully as doubt spread across her brow. "I'm sorry—"

"Where did they take her?" I demanded, gripping her shoulders a little tighter, but I eased off when she winced.

"I don't know!"

"Think. Surely you know something! You were here, weren't you? You saw her, you gave her that." I gestured with my foot at the giftbag in the closet.

"They sent me to my room," she answered quickly, holding her hands up. "I swear. Right as they started to argue they sent me away. All I heard after that were raised voices. I didn't do anything!"

"But you think your parents might have?"

She looked at first like she wanted to defend her parents, but her mouth set into a hard line. Her jaw twitched at the effort to keep still. She nodded, but furtively, like she knew she was betraying someone for the greater good.

"Were they alone?" I pressed further. I released her shoulders and took a tentative step back. She was on Danielle's side in this, which meant she was on mine—but she wouldn't be if I kept scaring her. "Was there anyone they were working with? Think hard."

"There was someone here early today, before Danielle arrived," she said, hugging her arms tightly and biting her lip. "Mam and da said he was a teacher, or mentor, or whatever for Danielle. I don't know. It was early in the morning, and I was avoiding being asked to help make breakfast..."

My first thought was Jeremy, but I stamped that idea out quick. After last year's ordeal, I couldn't see Jeremy working with witches *ever* again, even for revenge. That left the Agathati.

"Does a black triangle ring any bells?" I ventured warily.

She started to shake her head again, but her eyes sparked with recognition and she nodded. "Some books arrived for Danielle several months ago. There was a note with a black triangle…"

Meddling Agathati bastards. I dropped my head into my hands with a groan. *I guess it was too much to hope they'd all perished last year. What the hell do they want with her now?*

"Are you going to hurt me?" she asked after we were quiet for a moment. She shuffled her feet but didn't edge away. "Or use me as your hostage?"

"No," I answered honestly. My eyes skated over the forming bruises on her neck, from attempting to strangle her at first. *Fuck.* "And I'm sorry for earlier…"

"But you should," she said earnestly. At my incredulous look, she pushed off from the wall, practically hopping in excitement. "The hostage part, I mean. It'll get you to Danielle. We feck this place up and leave a little bit of *me* behind. I'm willing to give up a full fingernail. But hair is a little more menacing, you think?"

"You're way too into this idea," I said, deadpan.

"Because I'm angry!" She kicked at the silver knife she'd dropped in our scuffle, sending it skittering across the room. "My *parents*—who were nothing but complete *arses* to Danielle from the beginning—lured her here, abducted her, then lied to me about it. They let me go off with friends and didn't think to warn me that there might be a furious Lapsus on a rampage in our home when I got back!"

Despite my guilt and the anger still burning beneath the surface, a side of my mouth lifted and I let out a small huff of amusement. It was a terrible, negligent oversight of her parents not to warn her. Or had they assumed they'd be back by now? Was Danielle giving them more trouble than they expected? *That's my girl.*

"So yeah, I say we feck this place up even more, then you take me somewhere and leave behind something of mine, as a message," Caoimhe plowed on. "It serves them right, *and* it gets us to Danielle."

I chuckled again at her conviction. It could work if we weren't dealing with the Agathati. They didn't care about the innocents who got caught in their altruistic games.

"The witches they're with won't bargain," I told her after a beat, my shoulders dropping. "They have their prize. I'm sorry to say it, but they aren't going to give a shit whether I kill you or not."

"My parents will give a shit, though," she countered, pressing her fists to her hips and fuming with an indignation that *only* a young teen could. "Forget the others. My parents will absolutely trade me for Danielle. That's all we need."

She was right, and I kicked myself for it. If nothing else, ransoming Caoimhe would force the parents to tell me where Danielle was. All I needed was the location, and I could handle it from there without putting Caoimhe in any *real* danger.

Her phone was buzzing on the ground where she'd dropped it, but she stayed in place, with her hands on her hips. Her eyes held a ruthless challenge, and she tilted her head as if to say "your move."

I stepped over to the buzzing phone and brought the heel of my foot down on it with all my Lapsi strength. With a satisfying crunch, the phone practically flattened.

CHAPTER 18

DANIELLE

"**S**he's waking up," a voice said, some distance away.

"Finally," said another voice. The first had been familiar, but the second wasn't.

I tensed my hands into fists, but I couldn't move my arms further than that. They were bound to a pair of armrests.

Fuck, no. No, no, no...

I jerked my arms harder, but it was no use. My legs were bound at the ankles to separate chair legs, which was *different* from the previous cell. It quelled some of the panic, but not all.

Footsteps approached, and I forced my eyes open, expecting dark stone, chains, a dirty cot, and a big metal door. Instead, it was a bare concrete room with a cement floor that slanted gently to a drain in the center.

Warily, I tracked the man's movement toward me, not relaxing enough to breathe until I could see his eyes were an icy blue, not dark Kryrie eyes.

Mr. Flynn frowned by the door with his arms crossed, and most of my fear melted away. I didn't hold back the dark chuckle that bubbled up in my throat.

"You have no idea what you've done," I told him when my laugh subsided.

"Colm, leave us. Clearly your presence won't do us any favors," the stranger said, pulling a chair over from the wall.

Oh, yes, and you'll need all *the favors in the world to keep me from clawing your eyes out when you untie me*, I wanted to say, but I settled on glaring between the two of them instead.

Mr. Flynn left, slamming the door behind him. The stranger set the chair on the concrete ground two feet from me and took a seat. I studied him for a long moment while I waited for him to say something. He was the same man from that morning outside the Flynns' house. But more importantly, he wasn't Kryrie: just a mortal witch. I could handle that.

"Are you Agathati?" I asked, impatient after waiting for him to speak.

"Yes," he said, sitting back in his seat and looking at me calmly.

I sat heavily back in my seat with a groan and rolled my neck. "What do you bastards want with me now?" I demanded when I locked eyes with him again. Why me? I'd served my purpose as bait.

"We want you to change your mind on your current course of action," he said, idly rolling a phone over in his hand. "And we'd love to have someone with your talent on our payroll."

"My current course of action?" I repeated, rolling my eyes. I knew he meant Felkyn, but I *had* to be petulant. "What do you all have against me working on a Hollywood set as a makeup artist?"

He murmured something unintelligible under his breath and pressed his hands together, sandwiching the phone between his palms. He sat forward in his seat. "Do you have any idea how rare—how spectacular—your particular gift is?"

"Oh, I do," I assured him. My jaw twitched with the effort not to scoff at him again. "The Flynns never let me forget it.

They couldn't even teach me how to do the most basic things because they thought my magic was too *spectacular* to be deemed safe. So they dampened me, instead."

"That is...regrettable." With a sigh, he sat back and pocketed his phone. "A crime, really. You're truly special, Danielle, and you've been handled appallingly. We never would have sent you to them."

But you did.

"The Flynns aren't yours?"

He shook his head. "Christian found the Flynns for you on his own. Because he figured your usefulness to our organization was finished. And it would have been, but then we received word that a family was looking for a mentor for a fire witch. The first in a century. You were back on our radar, but we had to handle everything delicately."

"Because of my connections with Felkyn and the likelihood that I would go back with him?"

"And throw away this precious gift," he added, nodding again. "You have no idea just how useful your power is to us."

As a weapon, no doubt. I narrowed my eyes in annoyance. "You all *keep* saying that. Why not enlighten me?"

His mouth twitched, then flattened into a tight, humorless smile. "Not yet."

"You clearly know my history, so I really don't get what you're trying to do here. Abducting me, tying me to a chair, and sticking me in a cell-like room is *not* how you get me on your side." I tapped my toes on the concrete impatiently. "Seriously, it all seems a little...like you're setting a stage. *How* exactly is this supposed to change my mind?"

"Since you mentioned Hollywood, you can call me the *fixer*." He leaned an elbow on the armrest of his chair. His other hand slipped into the pocket of his slacks. "My specialty is changing or altering people's minds."

An involuntary snort escaped me. That sounded like something you'd only discover was your specialty if you were specifically training in offensive magic.

"It has plenty of uses, mainly in espionage or in negotiating and diffusing world-altering situations," he continued. "But mainly, *I* as a fixer change the problem's mind or make the problem disappear. I'm not going to kill you, but I will change your mind."

The threat would have rattled me, but my mind was still impervious to the exact magic he was threatening me with. A fragment of skeptical smugness must have flickered across my face because he tilted his head and regarded me with a cold smirk.

"You've proven to be a challenge, yes," he said, boring into me with his cold blue eyes. "I've been working on you for the past few hours and haven't been successful at getting in. Thankfully, I'm schooled in many methods." He pulled a capped syringe from his pocket and twirled it lazily between his fingers. His eyes never left my face, but mine were watching the syringe. "We just had to wait for you to wake up to try this next one. It's a little...cruder."

My stomach fluttered with wariness, but the door to the cell burst open. Before I could even wonder who'd barreled into the room, pain exploded across my cheekbone, snapping my head to the side and sending my ears ringing.

"Where is she?" Mr. Flynn shouted, grabbing fistfuls of my shirt and pulling me toward him. "Where's my Caoimhe!?"

"I've been here with you! How the fuck should I know?" I demanded, focusing on his red, terrified face, through the tears of pain that sprung to my eyes at the hard slap. But then my brain caught up with his words and wiped the defiant sneer off my face. "What do you mean where's Caoimhe?"

"She's gone!" he shouted, his hands still clutching my shirt like a lifeline. "Your Lapsus broke in and took her!"

"He would never do that!" I protested, shaking my hair out of my eyes.

"He did!" he insisted, his face inches from mine. "The house is all messed up, the front door's busted, her phone is smashed, and she's *gone*."

Dread stole the retort from my lips. Dread for Caoimhe and where she could be.

"He didn't do this," I said, finding my voice again.

"Yes, he did. He took my baby girl!"

"No, he didn't!"

While we continued back and forth, a pair of lackeys tried to pull the fuming man out of my face. Fixer stood from his chair and backed out of the way.

"Did you ever think it wasn't him, but *these* assholes?" I snapped.

He pulled his hand from his jacket pocket and held two things in front of my face: a phone and a lock of dark brown hair that hung in a kinked wave, like it'd been in a braid. *My* phone and Caoimhe's hair.

My argument was sucked back into my throat in a small gasp, because why would a kidnapper leave my phone if not to call it for ransom? Only a handful of people had my number who could have done this: Felkyn, or Caoimhe herself.

Behind him, Fixer had a glint of satisfaction in one of his pale eyes. *Is he gloating?*

"He won't hurt her," I said finally, but my voice shook.

Fixer grinned at the quake in my voice. *Yeah, he's definitely gloating.* But while it sounded like the quake in my voice was from doubt in Felkyn's innocence, it was more from *confusion*. Why would he do this? He knew the Agathati didn't care about casualties. Threatening Caoimhe wouldn't do anything to save me. Was he truly in a blind rage over my abduction? Or was Fixer gloating because it was what he wanted me to think?

"He won't hurt her unless something happens to me." I stumbled over the first few words but found my stride. "Let me go, and we'll talk to him. Because even though I believe in my heart that he won't hurt Caoimhe, I don't really know what he might do if I'm hurt."

"That's enough. I need my time with her," Fixer said, gripping Mr. Flynn's shoulder and pulling him back. The two lackeys fell back, and Fixer led Mr. Flynn toward the door. When they were halfway there, he spoke to Mr. Flynn in a low voice, but I could still hear him. "Normally, I'd be irritated at you bursting in here. But you've shaken her faith in her beloved, and she's scared. Now, is there any other insight you can give me into her psyche?"

Mr. Flynn glanced back at me, and I silently pleaded with him, despite the resentment between us. For half a second, I thought he was with me, but his face closed off and he turned back to Fixer.

"She's afraid of water."

Dread froze in my throat. What did *that* have to do with anything?

Fixer's back was to me, but I saw the muscles of his jaw lift into a smile.

"I can work with that." He stepped back from Mr. Flynn and motioned to the others in the room. "Don't let him out of your sight. I don't want him sneaking off to negotiate with this vigilante without us."

"But my daughter..." Mr. Flynn murmured, stopping at the door.

"We'll get her back as soon as we're done dealing with Danielle," Fixer said, though the coldness in his voice cast doubt on his sincerity.

Mr. Flynn looked back at me again, and I still pleaded with him silently. *Please don't do this.* A flicker crossed his eyes—but whether it was a flicker of guilt or of doubt at Fixer's promise, I didn't know. He let himself be led all the way out of the room.

Once the door closed, Fixer tucked his hands into his pockets and returned to the center of the room.

"Why are you wasting time with me when there's a *child* in danger?" I demanded, glaring at him.

"She's not my job," he said flatly. "My job is you."

"Fucking sociopath," I spat with as much venom as I could.

His mouth flattened and his icy eyes twitched infinitesimally. He reached toward me and brushed the hair out of my face. Before I could shudder away from the oddly intimate gesture, his other hand came around, holding the syringe. Without a word or a change in his cold expression, he jabbed it into my chest.

I cried out and tried to recoil from him, but he grabbed my hair and used it to keep me still while he pushed the plunger down on the syringe.

"I'm done playing *your* game," he muttered, staring down at me through narrowed eyes. "Now we play mine. So be a good girl and just *breathe*."

He pulled the syringe out of my chest and stepped back. I opened my mouth to demand to know what he'd just done, but I gasped involuntarily instead. Suddenly there wasn't enough air in the room to fill my lungs.

"What did—you—what—did—" I choked out between gasps. I gripped the chair's arms tightly as I tried to regain control of my lungs.

"I just gave your lungs a little boost to allow you to take in as much air as you can. It'll only last a few minutes," he explained, wheeling a small table over and positioning it by his chair. On it was a lit brazier, a glass bowl, and a number of ingredients: both liquid and powdered.

"Why?" I gasped out.

Two men stepped around me from behind. One attached a wired electrode to each of my collarbones, and the other attached two more to the insides of my wrists and clipped an oximeter to the end of my index finger. Another man wheeled a television cart into my peripheral.

"As I told you, I can't get into your mind, but I have other ways," Fixer explained, but he sounded off. I glanced back at him and realized his voice was distorted by the gas mask he'd strapped to his face while he mixed ingredients on the table. The other men were wearing similar gas masks. "This way is more work intensive but effective nonetheless."

"Someone needs to say it," I said, surprising myself that I was able to say the full sentence without gasping. "This is *not* the mask women refer to when they say 'the mask stays on.'"

"Jokes won't save you." He waved a hand dismissively and swirled the bowl around. "And just because you can crack wise when you're pinned down doesn't mean you're brave."

He pushed the wheeled table closer and ladled some of his mixture over the burning coals of the brazier. Steam billowed into the air with a quiet hiss.

"Is that what you say to all the girls you restrain and drug?" I quipped, but the moment was ruined when my lungs demanded more air, sending me gasping.

"So witty in a crisis," he mused, pouring more liquid onto the coals and sending clouds of steam into my face. "So fascinating. But rest assured. You might be a challenge, but you will not be my most difficult case."

"Why...why are you talking like a Kryrie?" I asked, my tongue working sluggishly. The room was spinning and seemed to be *changing*.

Distantly, I could hear Fixer's muffled laughter, but it sounded so far away. "Just breathe, pet."

I glanced around to find him still feet away, but with smoke and steam curling around him. His image twitched and doubled. I blinked, but it didn't help. Instead, he warped in front of me: the gas mask disappeared, his pale hair darkened and lengthened. And his eyes...

What the fuck?

I groaned and shut my eyes, ducking my chin into my chest while the air around me felt ready to crush me.

CHAPTER 19

DANIELLE

"**H**ey, pet."

My eyes snapped open at the familiar voice, because it *couldn't be.*

The man in front of me had shoulder-length, wavy brown hair. He would've been attractive if it weren't for his huge black irises: like a horse's eyes.

Alaric.

I tried to pull my knees up to my chest, but they were bound to the legs of a chair, and my wrists were bound to the armrests. *Fuck.*

"Did you miss us, Nineteen?" Karson asked. He circled around me and knelt in front of my knees.

My teeth chattered violently, making it nearly impossible to speak.

"It's not possible," I managed to choke out. "You're banished."

"We're hard to kill. Kudos on your little trick with the fire," Karson purred while he unfastened the restraints around my ankles. I whimpered involuntarily at his touch and sank back farther into the chair. "You know how much I adore fire."

"I hope you use your fire again. It'll make playtime that much more interesting." Alaric stared hard at me with his dark, horse-like eyes, but I couldn't look at him for more than a second without shuddering. When Karson moved away, Alaric darted forward and put his hands over my bound wrists, leaning into my face. "But, my, have we *missed* you."

This can't be fucking real. I pressed my eyes closed again. The walls were the same dark, wet stone I'd spent weeks staring at. But hadn't the boys blown up the lair when they rescued me? And how did I get here?

Alaric unbound my wrists and yanked me to my feet. I yelped at the sudden movement and stumbled into his chest. I reared back, but he held my wrists tightly in his clawed hands.

"We've been watching you, Danielle. We've been there in every single one of your nightmares that you try so hard to forget," Karson cooed, pressing himself against my back, his hands gripping my upper arms. "But to be back here in the flesh is...euphoric."

One of his hands cupped my jaw from behind. Their touches would be intimate if they didn't threaten violence with every motion.

"You've never *shared* me before, boys," I quipped sarcastically—it was that or go mad from the terror. "Are your figurative balls so blue from the long wait that you're willing to share—"

Alaric pressed his nails into my forearms. I clenched my jaw against the pain, and Alaric laughed. Behind me, Karson vibrated with the same laughter.

"Can you feel it, brother? Her spirit's been completely rebuilt from her time away," Alaric admired.

I hissed as he tore into my wrists with his sharp nails to emphasize his words.

"Yes, and even stronger than before. I can smell it in her blood," Karson agreed. He still held my jaw, and his middle finger toyed with the flesh of my cheek by my ear. "You have new tricks that will make this more fun than last time. And so do we."

His nail sliced into my cheek, and he dragged it downward, cutting me in a line from ear to jaw. This was new, and previously forbidden. They used to actively avoid leaving marks on my face because they liked how I looked. The scar through my eyebrow had been an accident from a stray lash of Grance's whip. What had changed their minds?

With a laugh, Karson released me and stepped back. Alaric whirled around, pushing me roughly away from him. I staggered and crashed to the floor. My elbow hit first with surprisingly little pain, then the back of my head smacked into the rough stone. Only it didn't feel like stone, it almost felt *padded*. Confused and jarred, I tried to move to sit up, but for a second I couldn't.

What the hell? As an experiment, I bumped my head against the floor again, and for just a second, the dark stone cell became a drab cement room with a drain in the floor, and the perspective was different: like I was still sitting in a chair.

This isn't real.

Alaric and Karson knelt over me, grinning like kids on Christmas. Alaric reached for my arm, but before he could grab me, I rolled to the side, into Karson's shins. In a blur of deep red hair, he toppled over.

I scrambled to my feet before Alaric could grab my ankles and drag me to him. If it was a drugged hallucination, did I have any control within it?

185

It will open. It will open. It will open outward, I chanted in my head as I dove for the door, willing my brain to manifest what I wanted. My shoulder hit the door with the full force of my momentum, and—against all logic—it budged outward. My teeth clacked together at the jarring impact, but it didn't hurt like it should have. The door groaned as I pushed against it, opening it farther until I could slip through it.

Outside was a hallway with weak yellow lights in the ceiling and pale cement walls. A hundred feet to my right was a staircase, leading up to the next floor. I had no idea if Alaric and Karson would follow me, so I sprinted down the hallway and up the stairs.

At the top was a steel door with a push bar and an illuminated exit sign above it. I put my whole weight into the push bar and barreled into whatever waited on the other side.

It was another hallway, this one more lit than the previous one, and it looked suspiciously like a hallway from my high school. With a small huff of amusement, I picked a direction and ran.

I skidded around a corner and crashed into a male chest, shrieking in surprise before I could recover. I tried to move around him to keep running, but he grabbed my upper arms and swung me into the wall of lockers.

"Hey, bitch!" His familiar voice singsonged maliciously, stopping me cold.

He had a permanently youthful face of twenty-something, with scowling brown eyes, thick brows, and straight brown hair that fell halfway down his back.

Jeremy.

"I see you're alive and well," he said flatly, staring down at me with annoyance. "I figured that much when I saw Colin's death announcement. Which—*Colin*, really?" He grimaced.

I tried to push him away, but he just huffed and pressed his leg between mine, pinning me to the wall of lockers with his hip. He forced my shoulders back into the lockers.

"I guess Felkyn pussied out on the sacrifice thing," he noted, his voice returning to deadpan. "Speaking of, how is the blond idiot anyway? I expected him to change you. Did he pussy out on that too? Or did you kick him to the curb?"

"Fuck off, you selfish, stupid prince," I spat, pounding a fist on his chest.

I jerked my knee upward into his crotch, but he hissed and jerked his legs back. He adjusted and pressed his forearm across my chest. He braced his other arm against my shoulder, where it connected to my neck.

"I'm afraid I've got to settle a score first." He leaned in close, and his brown eyes bored into mine with hatred.

"You're not real," I ground out through clenched teeth. I bucked again, swinging my fists at his chest. "You're not here. You're not real!"

"I'm not real?" He laughed, blocking most of my hits with his elbows. "Does *this* feel real?"

His palm struck the side of my jaw so hard my head snapped to the side and back into the metal locker with a clang. Stars speckled my vision and pain exploded in the whole left side of my face so sharply that my knees buckled. I'd have sunk to the floor if he wasn't pressing my shoulder into the wall.

"And look." He moved his hand from my shoulder to my throat and turned my head back toward him. "You're fucking bleeding."

He held his other hand up in front of my dazed face so I could see the smear of blood across his palm. I was still bleeding from where Karson had cut my face. Jeremy licked at the blood, and his face constricted with disgust as if the flavor offended him.

"Fucking witch. How did we *not* know?" he spat incredulously, wiping his hand clean on his green shirt. "Only good witch is a dead witch."

He gripped my neck with both hands and squeezed, cutting off my air.

It's not real. It's not real. It's not real. I kept repeating it in my head, not even bothering to fight Jeremy as he choked me. But my resolve failed when my lungs started to ache, and my chest shuddered. My face flooded with heat, and I beat my fists against his arms, trying to break his grip, but he held fast, his eyes boring into mine with all his hatred.

Dark spots dotted my peripheral, and my arms were losing strength. My vision was reduced to mere pinpoints, and my legs jerked uncontrollably. With a last gasp, I lifted my arm and placed my hand to his forehead. It was meant to be a slap, but instead my palm just rested there. Without meaning to, I reached in with my magic, like I'd done once to Jeremy, accidentally retrieving his deepest memories. Only this time, I didn't reach in with a hook, but with a knife.

He shrieked in pain and jumped back, gripping his head. I collapsed to my knees, gasping and coughing as my lungs reinflated and my body struggled to sort itself out. I put my hand to my throat and tenderly massaged it, wincing. This felt pretty fucking real.

I hadn't recovered enough to even crawl away when, with a growl of frustration, he hauled me back to my feet. He half-dragged, half-pushed me down the hall with him and into a room to our right.

This new room was dark and oddly reflective. He shoved me against a glass wall that divided it and stepped back.

Confused by the weird room, I stared around, putting my hands out and feeling around me. Another clear glass wall stood on either side of me, creating a cubby-like space that was about three feet by five feet. Was this a kind of mirror maze? When I backed away and turned to give Jeremy a questioning glare, a glass wall slid between us: closing me in a box.

Oh, no. I pressed a shaking hand flat against the glass. Dread and panic were fighting for the reins of my reactions. I stared out at Jeremy who still stood on the other side of the glass, gloating. *I feel like I've seen this movie...*

My horrified suspicion was confirmed when icy water crashed over my shoulders and chest from above, soaking me to the bone.

"No!" The word was half scream as I threw myself out from under the geyser-strength faucet and against the glass wall between me and Jeremy. "Don't do this! Anything but this!"

Jeremy just laughed and backed away out of sight.

CHAPTER 20

DANIELLE

The water was up to my knees impossibly fast, and it was so cold, my teeth were chattering. I blindly threw myself at every wall, banging on and clawing at the smooth glass surface. The water was higher than my hips and my muscles ached from the cold, but still I banged on the glass and cried out for anyone to hear me. The current, caused by my fevered movement through the water, jostled my footing, and I fell.

Instinctively, I gasped as I crashed beneath the surface and inhaled a mouthful of water. Somehow, I got my head back above the water, coughing and gasping desperately for air. My feet found the bottom, and my heart sank to find the water at chest level.

"Why are you doing this?" I screamed, looking around wildly for anyone outside the glass, watching me live my worst nightmare. "What do you want? I'll do it, just tell me what you want!"

My feet lost contact with the ground again, and I slipped beneath the surface before I could think to tread water and keep my head up. I resurfaced but couldn't touch the ground anymore. My head bumped the ceiling, and dread settled completely into my aching joints.

"No, no, no, no!" I shrieked, bracing my hands on the ceiling and leaning out of the torrential water pouring in. I hit my fists on the ceiling, but the force pushed me below the water again. I sputtered and tried to resurface, but there was no longer a surface. Distantly I heard the *thunk* of the hatch closing, and suddenly all was still. Air escaped me in little whimpers, even though I knew I needed to conserve as much air as I could. I slapped against the ceiling and the walls.

Let me wake up! I screamed silently, peering through the glass and slapping weakly at it. *I want to wake up now!*

My chest burned, demanding air. I didn't know how much time passed before my lungs seized and forced me to breathe in. Agony ripped through my chest and ignited in my nose. My muscles jerked and spasmed while everything fought for air that simply wasn't there. With every second, blackness spread across my vision, and as my muscles weakened, my panic rose to heart-stopping levels.

For a split second, my surroundings shifted and sensations changed. I wasn't weightless, but was soaked and lying down. A wet cloth covered my face, and the ice water crashed over it. Then the world shifted again, and I was weightless, floating inside a sealed tank.

My lungs were still spasming, but weaker now. Everything hurt, but distantly. I was going to die like this, trapped in a dream while my captors drowned me. A deep sadness settled into me, drowning out the agony in my lungs and limbs.

From down a long dark tunnel came a *thud*. Then another. And another.

My eyes cracked open in time to see a large fissure in the glass directly in front of me. And just beyond it, a blond angel swung again with inhuman strength at the glass. This time the glass spiderwebbed. But he was too late. I know I didn't close my eyes this time, but everything was dark. Dark. Silent. And pain-free.

A gony split my head wide open and I wanted to scream, but I couldn't make sound come out around the water my lungs were ejecting out of every orifice they could. Hands gripped my shoulders and helped me turn onto my side so I could better expel the water and eventually breathe in actual air.

"Oh thank god, Danielle!" I could barely hear him over my coughing and gagging. "I'm sorry! I'm so sorry it took me so long to get here!"

My lungs slowly settled, but everything hurt from a splitting headache to my inflamed throat, my bruised chest from being resuscitated, and my aching limbs. Despite the pain, and the lingering terror of having almost died, a heady rush of relief warmed my chilled skin. I tugged on Felkyn's shirt and dragged him closer to me so I could dive into his warm chest.

Staying wrapped in his arms, I turned my head to the side and took in my surroundings. When everything went dark, I'd been in a clear glass tank inside a dark, mirrored room. But Felkyn and I crouched in a room of pale cement with a metal grate in the center. No broken glass lay on the floor—only overturned buckets and a soaked towel. My back was against a heavy, padded chair, its restraints brushing my elbows.

Overturned tables and wires were strewn about, as well as bodies with varying incapacitating injuries. He'd killed or knocked out the Agathati bastards who'd tormented and ultimately drowned me. *Good riddance.*

"Looks like negotiations didn't go so well," I said, pulling out of his arms, but my wry smile faltered, remembering. "Wait—is Caoimhe okay?"

The relief in his eyes dissolved, and his brows knit together with regret. His jaw flexed as he swallowed hesitantly, but he didn't answer.

"Is she okay? Is she safe?" My throat was killing me, inside and out, and it hurt worse now that a terrified lump was forming in it.

"They...they wouldn't negotiate..." he choked out finally, his voice little more than a hoarse whisper. "And when they wouldn't, I lost control. I...I'm sorry. I'm so sorry..."

I sagged back against the legs of the chair as my chest felt like it was caving in. I hugged my arms, but then, despite everything, I leaned back into his chest. He stiffened, surprised, but then didn't hesitate to wrap himself around me, like I wanted him to.

I knew I shouldn't. I knew I should shy away from him and never let him touch me again. But right then I needed his arms. I needed his help holding in the pieces of me that were coming unglued, at least until we got out of there and I felt safe again.

A sob ripped from my throat, followed by a cry of pain I barely stifled. Everything was raw and throbbing. Every breath hurt, and my heart was breaking on top of it. Despite being grateful to be wrapped so tightly in his embrace, I pounded a fist once against his chest to show the anger buried deep beneath the exhaustion. His chest heaved beneath mine with a sorrow all his own.

"I'm so sorry, Danielle," he whispered as he nuzzled into my wet hair. "I...I fucked up. I fucked everything up."

He prattled on, apologizing profusely. But I could barely hear him over the blood pounding in my ears, reminding me too much of the horror I'd just escaped.

I'd been abducted and *drowned*. Caoimhe, my surrogate sister, was gone-murdered by Felkyn, my soulmate. My own kind despised me or wanted to use me. Why couldn't I have more than a few *weeks* of happiness at a time?

I still wanted Felkyn, and his love, but he was right. I could never forgive him for ripping Caoimhe away from me, and he'd never forgive himself. Deliriously, I wished I could split us both into two halves. One half of each could go off separately, taking all the anger and sadness and guilt with them. The other halves could stay together as we were supposed to.

I pressed my eyes closed and willed it away: willed everything away. With effort, the pounding in my ears lessened, and I could hear Felkyn's sorrowful murmurings again. Slowly, I pulled out of his arms and sat back, looking at him.

"I know you hate me. You should hate me. I don't deserve forgiveness for this." He ran his hands through his blood-streaked hair. "I know our life together is over, and with that, my life is over. I deserve to die."

I shook my head sadly. I couldn't reassure him with empty words, because he wasn't wrong. He didn't deserve to die, but forgiveness was a tall order.

"You should be the one to kill me." My face must have shifted subtly from indifference to a modicum of bewilderment because he plowed forward quickly. "Please. I don't want to live another day, let alone another thousand years with the guilt of killing another child. I've lived with it before, but add losing you on top of it...please, Danielle."

He took my hands and gently kissed the pads of my fingers, then pressed my palms to his chest, over his heart.

"Please, end it. It's a mercy."

Horrified by what he implied, I snapped my hands out of his grip. "That's not funny," I croaked hoarsely.

"I'm not trying..." He held his trembling hands up. "I've lost you. I've failed you. I can't go back to walking this earth alone. I deserve to lose you, but I don't want to *live* without you. *Do it.*"

"No. I won't!" I shook my head, hugging myself and tucking my fists between my arms and my sides.

"*You* will make it through this. You have before. You always come out so much stronger than before. My love, my phoenix." He put his hand to my cheek, and I was torn between leaning into it or batting it away. "You'll survive this. But I can't."

With a groan, I knocked his hand away and dropped my head heavily into my hands.

"I can't...I can't deal with this right now," I told him, massaging my throbbing temples. "Can we please just get out of here? Wherever here is?"

My brain and my body were exhausted. I'd been emotionally and physically tortured within an inch of my life. Every breath hurt because of my fatigued lungs, my bruised neck, and my abused ribcage. My nasal cavity burned, and every sniffle forced tiny water droplets into my airway, irritating it further. My joints and muscles ached from oxygen deprivation and from shivering.

We were still in this underground torture chamber, surrounded by dead or unconscious bodies of men who had drugged, tortured, and fucking killed me. And now he was begging me to kill him. It was too much for one day. All I wanted was a warm bed and sleep. Revenge could come later. But first we had to get out of there, and I didn't even know where we were.

My fingers stopped their circular rotation around my temples, caught on that last thought. How did Felkyn know where we were? He'd said they refused to talk to him. So how had he found me? And just in time to resuscitate me...

I slowly lifted my head from my hands, a question forming on my lips.

My eyes found his warm, pleading ones, but someone was standing directly behind him. Before I could react, a flash of silver slashed across Felkyn's throat and hot, red blood spouted forward like a geyser.

I screamed and jerked my hands up, as if it would stop the forceful spray from hitting me full in the face. Felkyn slumped forward, his head on my knee, and my scream morphed into a wail of horror. His hands twitched, searching for one of mine. Delirious from shock, I grabbed his hand and held on tight.

"My...phoenix..." he managed to whimper before another flash of silver arced through the air.

The knife plunged deep into his back, piercing his heart, and he dispersed into a cloud of dust. It coated me, sticking to my skin and clothes and flying into my mouth and throat as I inhaled to let out another scream. My chest convulsed in a fit that was half coughs and half sobs. My hands clawed at my eyes, scraping away blood and dust, and I lurched sideways, bracing my hands on the blood-stained cement, and retched.

The attacker was still there, but I couldn't be bothered to care. Let him fucking kill me, too. I was done. I had no more fight, no more care for my own life.

Gone. Everyone was gone. Felkyn was *gone*. My chest cleaved open, spilling everything I'd tried to push down at hearing about Caoimhe's death and his involvement. My eyes streamed. I gagged on dust and sputtered slobbery, mucusy blood back onto the floor. My fingers slipped in it, and I reared back onto my knees, wiping them on my shirt and trying desperately to wipe the blood from them. But it was no use. I was covered in it, and all my efforts just coated them in even more blood and dust—

No, not dust. Ash. Felkyn'd burst into a cloud of black and grey *ash*.

My...phoenix had been his last words.

Irrational laughter bubbled up in my raw throat, but I pressed my fists to my lips to keep it down.

Fuck you, Felkyn, for naming me phoenix. I was no phoenix. I wouldn't come back from this. I was broken beyond repair. They'd taken everything from me, and I had nothing left.

But deep within that aching despair was a rage that burned brighter every millisecond, wrapping around my innards and coating everything inside me with lighter fluid. I could ignite with a mere thought. *No, I mean, I* really *could ignite with a mere thought,* I reminded myself.

With another scream, the fire in my veins ignited and flame enveloped me, warming me, but not burning me or my clothes. Flames hissed off the liquid on the ground, and the blood sizzled and popped grotesquely, but I hardly noticed. I focused on the legs in front of me and lunged for them, wrapping my flaming arms around them.

The man shrieked in pain as his legs caught fire, and he crashed to the ground. I lunged again, and this time straddled his writhing, struggling body. It was Fixer. Of course it fucking was.

I savored the terror in his eyes as his body burned and continued to burn. Then with a roar that didn't sound human, I reached for his eyes and plunged my burning thumbs in.

CHAPTER 21

DANIELLE

"**F**ucking magnificent."

My eyes opened on a cement room that had previously been in disarray but was now undisturbed aside from the buckets strewn about. Fixer stood by his stupid brazier, having just lowered a lid onto it, choking the coals and trapping the hallucinogenic steam beneath it.

He and three other men stood watching me. It was hard to see their expressions through their gas masks, but I felt like some rare artifact on display.

Not me, though. My magic. My flames were what they found "fucking magnificent."

I let my fire die and sagged back onto my heels. I knelt in an area of dried cement, though outside that radius the cement was soaked with water. My nose, throat, and chest still hurt, as did my head and my joints, but I wasn't covered in Felkyn's blood, or ash, nor was the ground in front of me.

"Well done, Danielle," Fixer said beside me.

It might have all been a crazed hallucination—a beyond cruel one—but the rage it'd ignited was very, very real. I lunged to my feet, calling more fire up from the well inside me. Only nothing came. I could feel it swirling through my veins, but when I tried to reach for it, it shied away, just out of reach.

My legs gave out, and I sank back to the ground. Was I too tired to do it again? I'd never tried twice in one go before, so *maybe*. But Fixer's cold eyes held a measure of amusement as he stared down at me.

Two of the men moved beside me, each taking an arm. They helped me off the ground and back to the chair and sat me down. The restraints on the chair had burned away, and the chair cushion crackled beneath my legs.

"I stand corrected. You *were* my hardest case. But they all bow in the end, and you were no different," Fixer gloated in his emotionless voice while folding his undone sleeve up to his elbow.

One of his lackeys held up a paper cup to show me two pills that I recognized as name-brand pain reducers, so I took them willingly. I choked them down dry because I couldn't bear the idea of drinking water after almost drowning in it.

The other pulled an IV over and sanitized the inside of my elbow. I jerked a little in protest, but he assured me it was just electrolytes to rehydrate me.

I watched him insert the needle and hook up the hose, but my eyes strayed to the inside of my wrist. I had a tattoo of two hearts there, but above them were outlines of three crescents in raised pink flesh, like a healed brand; the same decorated my other wrist. I recalled Alaric digging his nails into my forearms in the vision: it must have been when they did this to me.

"What...what is this? What was the point of that whole show?" I asked when the lackeys stepped away from me. I rubbed my thumb against my chin, feeling the sharp pain cut through my jaw. My thumb came away with a small streak of fresh blood on it.

"We've bound your magic with a spell. Your precious permanent shield around your mind is still as strong as ever, but you won't be able to craft any new magic unless we want you to. A temporary measure, we hope, until we can trust each other and you agree to work for us. Your gift is too valuable to let you squander it, so we'll control it until you can be trusted to use it," he explained, expressionless. "And the mindfuck was because we needed you to *choose* to use your magic first before we could bind it."

"You tormented me with my demons. You *drowned me*. You made a farce of killing Felkyn...just to manipulate me into setting shit on fire? You could have just asked!" I shook my head, and my fists clenched over my knees. "And after all that, you want me to work for you? That'll never happen."

"We'll see about that." His lips turned up into a one-sided smirk and he ran his thumb down a matching set of crescent brands on the inside of his wrist without breaking eye contact with me.

The magic I'd been unable to tap into moments earlier ignited in my wrists, and flames encircled my arms but swept downward and gathered in my palms. My stomach trembled with horror, knowing I wasn't doing this—*he* was.

I recovered from the shock of having my ability hijacked and curled my fingers, calling the magic back into my veins. I even tried thinking soothing thoughts at the licking flames. Nothing worked. I had zero control over my own magic.

The flames from my right hand leapt to my left, and the combined flame arced high into the air.

"It's absolutely stunning." He stared at the long willowy flame as it waved lazily in the air with the threat that it could easily become a fire whip. "Oh, the things we could do, and the plans we have. But for now..."

He raised his arm and, horrifyingly, the flame arced toward his outstretched hand. There was a tug on my wrists, as if he was pulling a thread from the veins there, and I gasped. I clenched my fist and pulled my arms in tight, groaning at the discomfort of having the magic pulled from me. The long arc of flame stretched between us, curling into a condensed ball in his hand. When it was to his liking, he released me, and I collapsed against the chairback, shaking violently from the effort.

"And she's stunned into silence, at last," he jabbed, grinning at me with an icy sneer while he held the pilfered bit of *my* magic in his hands.

He turned the condensed fireball between his hands, admiring it like it was a precious diamond the size of a softball. He stared for one more moment, then turned and tipped it into a glass jar and screwed on a lid. From the barely distinguishable blue iridescence in the otherwise clear glass, I assumed it was enchanted to preserve the fire inside as well as not heat the container.

Fixer sat in his chair with the jar on his lap, and he scooted forward, shortening the distance between our knees.

"You've got what you wanted from me, so can you please just leave me alone now?" I demanded softly. I was cradling my shaking hands against my chest, phantom sensations were tickling my veins, like marching ants. The painkillers were working and the ache in my head and joints was dissipating, and the supercharged electrolytes were helping ease the muscle fatigue, but mentally, I was tapped out. "I'm at capacity for bullshit. And right now, it feels like you just cut off one of my toes and are preparing to taunt me with it!"

"A toe," he repeated in an incredulous hiss. He tapped his fingers impatiently on the jar's lid. "When you work with us formally, you'll *appreciate* the kind of magic you have and how important it could be."

He leaned forward in his chair so his face was closer to mine, his eyes flashing with barely contained impatience.

"Your magic, your special, anomalous gift isn't just fire. It's witch's fire. The best weapon outside of silver against Lapsi, and something many of us believe is the thing that can kill Cain."

I groaned and rolled my eyes. *Not this fucking topic again.*

"There's a legend among witches about the coming of someone who doesn't fit any mold. Who presents with anomalies. And it's believed that this witch will be the key to killing the Original Lapsus and ending Kryrie everywhere."

"Tell me you don't think I am witch Jesus. I can't take that right now." I rolled my eyes furiously.

"You, Danielle, are a petulant, hard-headed bitch. Not *witch Jesus*," he hissed, his fingers tightening on the glass. "But you *are* an anomaly. You're not even half-blooded—a quarter at most. And you grew up apart from the witch community. This was too intriguing to let you get away without studying you. The first fire witch in a century. That alone makes you an amazing asset for the Agathati, but everything else makes you an *invaluable* asset, and we can't let all that potential go to waste."

With a growl, I lunged at him, my hands clenched into claws, but his lackeys grabbed me and pulled me roughly back into the chair. I brought my knees up and tried to leverage my body forward, but they were too strong. A wide belt was pulled across my chest and tightened, securing me once again to the chair, with my arms pinned to my sides.

"But until you can keep that temper under control and prove we can trust you, this spell stays. We decide if and when you use your magic, and even then, we'll direct it, or take it and store it." He leaned an elbow on his chair arm, stroking his chin thoughtfully.

"So, it's to be slavery," I said with a humorless smirk.

"A temporary arrangement. You've proven that you can be broken and bent to our will. It's difficult but doable." The fingers of his other hand tapped idly on the lid of the jar. "And what broke you was seeing your precious Felkyn die. I think that's what we'll use *this* for. Cutting your ties completely with that Lapsus will be another step toward your partnership with the Agathati."

Before the horror of his words could fully sink in, the door to the room opened and another lackey burst in.

"The Lapsus is calling. For ransom no doubt," he said, holding my phone out in front of him.

Fixer didn't turn, but kept his eyes on mine while his face broke into a chilling grin.

"Perfect timing."

CHAPTER 22

DANIELLE

"**S**o, where are we going anyway?" I asked Mr. Flynn, staring at the trees and looking for any landmark that looked familiar. "Are we even still in Ireland? How long was I out the first time? Were we traveling that whole time, or are we still in Bray?"

I'd been pestering them with questions the whole ride, mostly to annoy Mr. Flynn who was trying hard to pretend I didn't exist. Beside him sat one of Fixer's lackeys, with bulky headphones covering his ears and—in true bad-guy-lackey fashion—dark sunglasses obscuring his eyes. I sat facing them, my hands bound at the wrists by black cord and looped over the grab handle above the car's window. My arms were tingly from being elevated for so long, but at least I was moderately comfortable and in dry clothes. It was just a pair of black sweats and a gray T-shirt, but it was better than sitting in wet jeans forever.

"Does Felkyn think he's meeting just you?" I tried again after being quiet for a moment.

Mr. Flynn's eyes rolled skyward, probably because he'd assumed I was done asking questions.

"Or does he know there's a whole party coming to the meeting?" I continued, shifting my gaze between the two of them. Mr. Flynn avoided my eyes and the lackey—let's call him *Jim*—remained silent and impassive as ever. "I'm betting the first one, because you wouldn't want him knowing he was walking into an ambush..."

I was sure Felkyn knew it was all a setup. He knew the Agathati didn't bargain. But if he'd agreed to something, I wanted to know what it was so I could anticipate his plan. Because he had to have a plan: he couldn't expect *me* to have a plan. *Then again, he doesn't expect you to be completely cut off from your magic.* The thought rattled me. It was possible he was counting on my magic to assist him in some way. *Fuck*.

"Whatever the plan is, I'm sure Felkyn's thinking about Caoimhe's safety above everything else," I continued with a lofty shrug. "I can't say the same about these assholes."

I glared at Jim, but he seemingly didn't hear me over the music he was blasting in his ears. Were I his boss, I'd reproach him for being unprofessional and not paying attention to his prisoner, but as his prisoner, his dissociation could really only *help me* at this point. Hell, his head was even nodding a bit, like he was dozing off. *Incredible, Jim.*

"I envy your unshakable faith in this Lapsus and that he hasn't already hurt Caoimhe," Mr. Flynn noted, speaking for the first time since we'd gotten into the van and he'd protested being made to sit across from me.

"And I envy your naïve faith in these guys," I shot back at him, jerking my head in Jim's direction. "I don't, actually. They're bastards, and I don't want to have faith in them."

"I can't wait for this whole thing to be over so I can finally be done with you and your need to be contrary about everything." He sighed, rolling his eyes again in frustration.

"Yes, *so* contrary about everything, especially about being sold into slavery," I quipped, matching his tone. "How you live with it on your conscience is beyond me."

"I don't need to justify anything to you. And conscience?" He looked at me sharply. "Nothing will be on my conscience because I won't remember this at all. I'll barely remember *you*."

"What...what do you mean?" I wanted to scoff at him, but the confidence in his statement had my stomach clenching with dread.

"What did he say he was?"

"A fixer..."

"And a fixer solves a problem..."

"Or makes the problem disappear?" I finished for him, remembering Fixer's words from earlier.

"When he's done fixing the problem, it disappears, and so does he," he explained calmly, leaning forward. "He's a ghost story. He wipes all memory of him from people's minds. He wears a charm that prevents his face from sticking in people's memories. Even those who work for him don't remember everything.

"When this is over, and it's time to return to base, he'll wipe you from our minds, as much as he can. You'll be the witch we housed for a week or so, nothing more. He'll do the same to anyone who knew you too, so you can properly disappear into the folds of the Agathati."

Anyone who knew me. My brain kept repeating the words, and each time they held more weight.

How far did that extend? Caoimhe? Aoife? Shauna? My bosses in L.A.? Anyone who would look for me wouldn't know to look for me. It was like the Kryrie, just less destructive. I'd be erased completely. Again.

"What did I do to you to make you hate me enough to let these people enslave me?" I asked, my voice small and flat.

"You're hardly enslaved," he muttered with a scoff. Yet he diverted his proud eyes from mine. "You're just willful and need to be tamed before they can work with you."

"They bound my magic so I can't use it unless *they* want me to. They stole some of it and intend to use it against a Lapsus they don't know," I argued helplessly. "And I'm the only one here truly scared that Caoimhe is going to get caught in the crossfire."

"The whole point of this"—he gestured impatiently at the van around us—"is to get her back. They're negotiating to get her back."

"It isn't negotiating when they don't intend to bargain," I snapped. "They're not going to trade *me* for *her*. It's not a negotiation, it's a trap."

He shook his head incredulously.

"Look, I get it," I said levelly. "You're eager to be done with me, with them, with this. Eager to get back to life in a sleepy city with your wife and daughter. But you're thinking too far out. Focus on the now, and the very near future. Because if you don't, you're going to be utterly fucked."

As expected, he turned angrily to me at my crass language. I caught his eyes with mine and bored into them, begging him to *listen* to me.

"Do you know what they took from me?" I asked him before he could look away again. "They essentially have a bomb. They want to use it on Felkyn, and they want me to see it, because it will destroy me. Now, map this out in your brain. Imagine where everyone is standing in this scenario. They want Felkyn in the blast radius and me as far from it as possible. Where is Caoimhe in this?"

I paused long enough to watch his expression change. He was calculating it in his head, mapping it out like I asked.

"He wants them to hand me over, and they have no intention of doing that. So he'll be clinging tight to his human shield. This isn't my first hostage situation with the Agathati, and my experience tells me they aren't going to make sure Caoimhe's out of the way before they lob that bomb his way." I flicked my gaze over at Jim to see if he was going to step in and silence me or argue with me. But he gave no indication that he was listening at all. "Now, if you can still sit there totally confident that their intentions suit *your* interests, I'll stop wasting my breath."

I waited, but he said nothing. His expression closed and his jaw tensed, and he turned his face away and stared out the car window. I shut my eyes and leaned back in my chair, bumping my head on the seatback.

Had I really expected him to back me up? He'd always been a hard-headed person, determined to hate me. Whereas Mrs. Flynn, while she didn't like me either, had never been horrifically unkind. She'd left me alone, yes, but she'd never left me to fend for myself. She washed my clothes with everyone's. I was always invited to the dinner table, or a plate was always made for me and left at my door. She bought makeup remover for my makeup experiments with Caoimhe and even complimented me on the results.

I'd have greatly preferred sharing a car ride with her than her husband. *She* I could have persuaded to my side because I just wanted to save Caoimhe.

"Where's your wife?" I asked him, opening my eyes again and peering at him.

He glanced at me but quickly turned away again, almost as if the look had been involuntary.

I struck something. I thought back to the house, just before he and Fixer drugged me. She'd been telling them to stop.

"She doesn't approve of any of this, does she?" I asked, fighting back the smirk creeping across my lips. "Oh, and I bet she's *beyond* pissed at you because it's threatened Caoimhe. You...you're hoping she'll *conveniently* forget all of this."

Silence. But he wouldn't look at me, so I knew I was right. He was ensnared in this and banking on Fixer *fixing* whatever marital problems came after either the loss of a child or, best case scenario, a husband's rash actions.

I rested my forehead against my forearms dangling from the grab handle. *Felkyn has a play. He has a play. I don't need a play*. I tried to convince myself, but it was nagging at me. Why was Felkyn using Caoimhe as a hostage when he knew the Agathati wouldn't play ball? Or was he really expecting me, the prisoner, to be the one with the play? Damn it!

"If his magic is anything like Lapsi mesmerism, it won't erase everything," I told him, lifting my head again. "If Caoimhe dies in this, they can't erase it all. Even on the off chance she lives, he can't wipe away all the anger, the resentment, the *trauma* of your betrayal. You might not lose them in the aftermath once I'm taken away and it's all forgotten, but I bet you'll lose them in other ways."

I was quiet while I let that sink in. I watched him but also watched Jim, making sure he was still ignoring us. His facial expression hadn't changed, and his head still lolled a bit. He was definitely nodding off. *You're a shit lackey, Jim, but I'm not complaining.*

"But a way to win their favor back is if you help me out of this," I said quietly, looking past them both, out the back of the van. No one was following us, so were we at the back of a convoy? How close were the other vans? "Please?"

"How would I even?" he asked in an exasperated whisper, looking around wildly, as if for a mic.

"Are we following another van?" I asked him. Since he was facing the front of the van, he could see better than I could.

He looked past me and shook his head. "We were, but they're pretty far ahead of us. You have a plan?"

"I'll make them stop, then make a run for it," I explained, looking Jim over and confirming that he wasn't wearing a gun or a taser. "I can outrun all of you, even with my hands tied. I'd prefer to drive, but *I* don't know how."

I looked at him pointedly to make sure he got my meaning. He glanced at the driver, upfront, and with a sigh, he gave a small nod. Hopefully that nod meant he'd take care of the driver while I ran for it.

I lifted my wrists from the grab handle and hit my fists on the ceiling of the van to wake Jim and get the driver's attention. I exclaimed that I needed to pee, immediately, or else I was going to get messy. It didn't take much to convince them: just reminding them of the IV push they'd stuck into me and the amount of water I'd ingested in their torture. The driver begrudgingly pulled the van into a small gas station.

Jim leaned over and opened the van door, shifting his weight precariously so he could unhook the length of cord from the grab handle. I took only a second to relish the relief of lowering my arms before I brought my elbow up into his temple.

The hit was hard, but not as hard as my tingly arms could have normally managed, probably. I turned and booked it away without a backward glance. Behind me, I heard the thud of his knees against the van's floor, knocked off balance by my surprise hit.

I wasn't a competitive sprinter anymore, but I was still fast, even with my hands tied. I sprinted away, past the small gas station, and hooked immediately behind it, praying he hadn't seen me turn. As soon as he came into view around the corner, I kicked out, hard, at his knee, bringing him to the ground. I looped my bound wrists around his neck and climbed onto his back.

"See how you like it, fucker," I hissed in his ear, while his protests became weaker. As soon as his body slumped forward, I released him, and backed away. I grabbed his phone and thought about keeping it but decided to smash it instead. I tentatively jogged back around the building as Mr. Flynn pulled an unconscious lackey from the driver's seat onto the pavement. I grabbed for his phone, and a familiar chemical odor reached my nostrils.

"You had more of that stuff?" I demanded, gagging. "We could have used it on Jim, too!"

"Jim?" he asked, confused as he climbed into the driver's seat.

"It doesn't matter now," I snapped, throwing the driver's phone to the pavement as hard as I could.

Once we were back on the road, I ran my bound hands through my hair, trying to think quickly. The jailbreak had worked better than I expected, but what was my next move?

"I need a phone," I demanded.

"Yours is with Fixer," he explained, handing me his from his back pocket.

"It's fine, I memorized the numbers."

"You calling Felkyn?"

"Hah, as eager as I'm sure you are to kick his ass for abducting Caoimhe, no," I told him, while the call dialed out. "I'm sure they've got your phone tapped anyway, so they'll see your records later. No, I'm keeping them on their toes and calling someone they don't expect."

It rang four times and went to voice mail, unsurprisingly. Who answers an unknown number? I dialed again.

"Riley. I need you," I said when he finally picked up.

CHAPTER 23

FELKYN

"Riley, as thrilled as I am that you've unblocked me, this is not a good time—"

"No, it's a good time. If you're not somewhere safe, get there," he snapped on the other end of the line.

I stopped pacing and glanced around wildly, struggling to switch gears from panic to conversation.

Through gritted teeth, I said, "I'm somewhere safe, now what—"

"And Caoimhe?"

"How do you know about Caoimhe?" I demanded. I glanced inside the small arcade, where she was trying to guide a claw above a bunch of plushies.

"Where are you? I'm coming there."

"The Queen Mary, Long Beach, California. We're on the main floor," I explained, swallowing my surprise at his bossy tone. *What the hell is going on?*

"Smart," he acknowledged and hung up.

The Queen Mary was a retired, permanently docked cruise ship. I'd chosen to hide Caoimhe there because it was entirely surrounded by water but was just six feet from land. It would confuse the hell out of anyone trying to use a tracking spell to find her. Plus, it was haunted, and that had intrigued Caoimhe to no end.

I'd only been back from the farce of a negotiation for a few minutes and had distracted Caoimhe with a walk to the ship's little arcade. While she played, I'd been stewing over what I'd witnessed and what it *meant*.

I got there early and parked on the roof of a nearby building to scope the area ahead of the meeting. Mr. Flynn had agreed to come alone, but I wasn't surprised when a black van pulled up and half a dozen men piled out. Mr. Flynn was absent, and the man in charge was nondescript with pale features and glasses. And there was no Danielle.

They seemed to be waiting for more to join them, but no other van showed. The pale man paced back and forth, then walked away from the van and lifted his phone to his ear. He tried calling three people; on the last one, his back went rigid and he ripped the phone away from his ear and peered down at his wrists.

"No!" he screamed and sprinted back to the van.

Past him, inside the van, I could see a large glass jar with an orange glowing ball inside. As he scrabbled to get a grip on it, the glow diminished. By the time he pulled it from the cab, the light vanished completely.

He let out a string of curses and hurled the jar. It shattered on the pavement, and I couldn't help the chuckle that escaped my lips. I didn't know what was in that jar, but anything that upset them was a win in my book.

But now that I was back and thinking it over, I had a sinking feeling that it'd been somehow connected to Danielle. It dying couldn't mean that she was gone. It just couldn't.

Only a moment passed before Riley stomped into the lobby, looking all business in a black button-down tucked into belted black slacks. His hair was messy but looked like it'd been styled fairly recently.

"Hey, man, you going to explain, or do I have to hug you..." I asked him as he approached, but I faltered as the smell of a club and stale beer hit my nostrils.

"She in there?" he said by way of greeting, angling to move around me into the arcade.

"Hold on, hold on!" I sidestepped, blocking his path and holding up my hands. "I'm happy to see you, but this vibe you're giving off is weird. I'm not letting you near her until you explain yourself. And you...did someone throw a *beer* at you?"

The damp fabric of his left shoulder was the source of the stale smell. His hair even glistened with it a little. *The hell?*

"It's a common occurrence at my work." He shrugged.

"Work?" I scoffed automatically, my mouth twisting into a confused sneer. Everything about Riley right now contrasted his usually docile demeanor and sloppy, emo wardrobe.

"Yes, work. I'm a bouncer at a club, protecting the dancers and ejecting men who get too handsy," he explained airily, gesticulating impatiently. "And Danielle called me away from that. Before you freak out, she's *safe*. She's making sure *you're* safe, by asking me to deliver Caoimhe to her father."

"Why didn't you lead with that?" I demanded, grabbing his arms. "How? Where?"

I wanted to fucking kiss him, but he backed away.

"I'm sure she'll explain, but she called me from Caoimhe's dad's phone, had me meet them on the side of the road in Ireland and take them to Andre's house. From there, I took the dad to collect the mom, and now *they're* in a safe location because they have to lay low from the Agathati. Now, did you really abduct a *child*?"

"Abduct is a strong word." I smirked, able to joke now that I knew Danielle was alive and safe. "Really, all I did was take her on a fun trip to a haunted cruise ship..."

"All right, sure." He rolled hie eyes and looked past me into the arcade. "I'm supposed to get Caoimhe to her parents. Andre will be setting them up somewhere with heavy wards, but right now, he's protecting Danielle beneath *his* wards until you can get there."

"Caoimhe, come here!" I called over my shoulder, resisting the urge to shift to Italy immediately. She hurried to my side. "Caoimhe this is my friend Riley, he's—"

"The drummer!" she said excitedly, bouncing on her heels. "She's told me so much about you! And I've listened to the band *so many* times!"

"Heh, thanks." Riley ran a hand through his reeking hair in his discomfort. "I wish I could say she told me a lot about you, but I've been kind of under a rock for a year, so—"

"I want to be a drummer, too!" she interrupted him, hopping from foot to foot with young teenage energy. "I watch you in the live performances all the time, and kind of try to follow, but I don't know what I'm doing, and I don't have a set..."

His uncomfortable expression split into a wide, pleased grin, and he glanced at me with knowing eyes. He leaned down to her.

"I'll buy you a set, as soon as I can," he told her, still grinning. "That will surely annoy the hell out of your parents.

Not the punishment that they deserve, but you get what I mean."

"Caoimhe, you're going to go with him to your parents because they aren't my biggest fans," I told her, after she squealed with delight at the promise of a drum set. She nodded and stepped over to Riley's side. "Give them hell for me, though, okay? And sorry again for the bruises..."

Andre was outside his house when I arrived beyond his perimeter. No doubt he was adding more wards to his already fortress-like array.

"She's inside, door's unlocked." He waved at me but didn't look up from his spell casting. It was after dark, so he had to squint to see what he was doing in the dim porch lighting.

Danielle was seated on a couch facing the door when I entered, with a mug of honeyed tea between her hands and her knees bouncing anxiously. She quickly put the mug aside and stood on shaky legs as I crossed the room to her, and her shoes squelched wetly as she put weight on the soles.

I pulled her into my arms, squeezing her as tightly as I could without crushing her. She buried her face in my chest and wrapped her arms around my waist, pulling me closer, as if nothing would be close enough. After a moment, I loosened my hold and ran my hand up and down her back while she grabbed fistfuls of my shirt and pulled it to her nose. She inhaled deep and let it out in a long sigh.

"Caoimhe's okay. And I'm sorry I had to use her," I said, running my fingers through her damp, tangled hair. "Would you believe me if I said she put me up to it?"

Her laugh was a soft huff against my chest, and her shoulders shook once. Finally, she pushed herself away from my chest so she could look up at me, her eyes shiny and brimming with tears.

"Yeah, I would, actually," she said with a smirk. "I bet it was her idea. But she doesn't know the Agathati like we do—no one does, it seems."

The good humor faded between us as I held her shoulders at arm's length and assessed the damage. Her hair was damp and tangled, her face was pale and haggard, and dark shadows circled her eyes. There was a shallow cut on her jaw, and the area around it was bruised. Bruises also circled her neck, similar to Caoimhe's after I'd nearly strangled her.

I turned her face up and put my lips to the cut on her jaw, working it with my tongue until it started to bleed again. My saliva would heal it and the bruise in no time.

Once that was done, I lowered my hands from her shoulders, down her arms, but stopped at the bandages over both of her wrists. I lifted them and turned them between us, inspecting them. I hissed at the fresh blood dotting the bandages.

"Leave those alone," she said sharply, pulling her wrists from my hands and cradling them against her chest. "Those need to heal on their own and scar. They're Andre's handiwork."

"What?" I demanded, shocked. "Why?"

"They branded me with binding spells—*and* a tracking spell. He had to cut into them and mar them to break their hold," she explained carefully, flexing her fingers as she spoke. "They wanted me to work for them but knew I wouldn't come willingly. They bound my magic so I couldn't use it, but first I had to choose to use it. So they..."

She looked away from me. I was dying for her to tell me everything, but I waited to see if she'd continue on her own before I pressed.

"They couldn't get into my mind, so they instead did a lot of psychological manipulation...there were drugs involved...and waterboarding..."

Fuck. I ran my hands down my face in silent exasperation. She backed away and sank back onto the couch, hunching forward so her elbows rested on her thighs.

"And once they bound me, they could make me use my fire whenever *they* wanted. Until I was fully indoctrinated. Not only that, they..." She ran her hands through her hair in frustration.

Andre entered the room, but he didn't say anything. He walked silently to an armchair in the corner and sat down.

"They took some fire from me against my will," she continued after nodding to Andre in acknowledgment. "And they were going to use it as some kind of grenade or bomb. They wanted it for *Cain*."

Her voice dripped with disdain when she said his name. I rolled my eyes at the selfishness of their plan, because *of course*.

"But first, they wanted to use it on you. They wanted me to watch them destroy you. And I already watched you die *once* today. I couldn't do it again."

Her words came out in a rush, and my brows knit together, wondering just what they'd made her see while torturing her. After pausing for a few seconds, she let out a shaky laugh.

"So, I'm sorry for kind of hijacking your plan, but I didn't want to let them use my magic to kill you, and I didn't want

Caoimhe to end up in the line of fire—literally. I found a way to convince Mr. Flynn to help me save her."

"I wouldn't have let her get hurt," I told her, shaking my head. I backed up to a chair facing her and sat down. I would've gotten Caoimhe out of there at the first sign of danger and come right back. "It was a bad plan, though. Yours was better."

"Andre—" she looked down at the bandages on her wrists "—in disabling the binding spells, did it dispel the fire they were holding?"

"I...I really don't know," he answered, shaking his head. "It's possible it destabilized or merely died away. Or it's possible he put some of his magic into it, which stabilized it even after not being connected to you anymore. So little is known about fire crafting—"

"It did," I cut in, recalling the fire in the glass jar dying and him shattering the container. "I saw it go out. Probably right as Andre cut the connection. It's not a threat anymore."

"Thank god," she breathed out, her whole body sagging from the relief. She rubbed her palms into her eyes for a moment, then lifted her head and fixed me with a determined look. "There's just one more thing to do then. I need you to make me a Lapsus. Tonight."

"What?" I recoiled in my seat. "No, we said we weren't in a hurry for that—"

"That was before I realized my magic can be used against my will and taken from me. I don't want to give them a chance to do that ever again, so we're doing it tonight."

Andre cleared his throat uncomfortably and leaned forward in his seat. "Danielle, you know that with your mind protected, it's going to—"

"Hurt. I know. I'm fully aware of that," she told him, frustration seeping into her voice. She ran her hands through her hair again. "I know it's going to be hell. But they don't want me to be Lapsi, so fuck them, that's exactly what I'm going to be."

———

She turned down my offer of a last meal, and instead we headed straight to Aoife and Declan's new place. They'd recently moved across Ireland to the larger city of Limerick. It was a good place to hide, and it comforted her to be close to her favorite people in the transition.

"I know we tested this once before, just to see, but this will be worse," I told her, even though I knew she didn't need me to say it. "And I don't know if Aoife's stuff will have any effect..."

"I know," Danielle said, tightening her shoulders in a way that told me she was trying to hide her annoyance. "It can't be worse than drowning, or thinking you're drowning, when you're really being waterboarded..."

"It might—"

"Shut up. I'm not backing down from this. And I'm not scared of a little pain." She grabbed my hand and held it tightly, putting her other hand to the side of my face so I couldn't look away from her. "You know what they did to me? They attacked me with my worst fears. The Kryrie, a revenge-seeking Jeremy...drowning. The last one was of you dying in front of me. But *this* wasn't one of those fears. I'm not afraid of the pain or of what's on the other side. I want this."

And I wanted it too. I just hated that it was going to be agonizing.

"We're standing by, should you need anything," Aoife piped up from the desk where she and Declan were nervously arranging her concoctions. "I know your stubborn ass will refuse anything for the pain, but I have options ready just in case."

"I'll hold off as long as I can." Danielle threw her a feral grin in jest. "But thank you."

"And please, try to keep the screaming to a minimum," Aoife added. "If you wake Libby, I will never forgive you."

"I promise. I'm not a screamer, usually." Danielle scooted closer to me on the guest bed so she was seated sideways between my spread legs and her legs draped over my right one. My hands went to her hips, pulling her closer, and her arms curled against my chest. All I had to do was lean my head down and my lips would be at her throat. She gave me a last smirk and said, "Felkyn, with respect. *Bite me.*"

"You've been practicing that one since you met me, haven't you?" I asked her, but I didn't wait for an answer. I swallowed my dread at hurting her and pressed my lips to her neck.

She tensed as I started to drink, but she didn't go rigid immediately. Her hands clenched fistfuls of my shirt, and she breathed as evenly as she could through the pain. Her shuddering breaths kept me from giving in to the high that her witch-enhanced blood gave, even though I could feel my mind going fuzzy at the edges. No matter how good she tasted, this wasn't something I wanted to enjoy. This was a task.

Last time, we'd done only five seconds, and she'd nearly screamed at the end of it. She lasted longer than five this time before she let out a pained whimper and her back arched away from me. I wrapped my arm around the back of her head and clasped my hand to her mouth so she could wail as loudly as she wanted and kept going. I had to keep going, but it was getting difficult, even for me.

She writhed, trying to wiggle away from me, but I held on. Her legs bucked as she twisted in my grip, and I pushed down hard on her thigh to keep her from squirming. Her fists clenched tighter and beat against my chest. Damn it, it wasn't enough yet. I had to keep going.

She squealed against my hand and pushed her clenched fists hard against my chest. With a gasp, I pulled my face from her neck and dove away from her. But the intoxicating quality of her blood stole all manner of grace from me, and I toppled sideways off the bed, nearly face-planting.

Above me, Danielle fell forward onto the bed, pressing her forehead and her fists into the mattress while she let out a long frustrated moan.

"Fuck...I'm sorry." She groaned into the bedspread. She shook herself but didn't sit up immediately. "We can go again, I just need a minute..."

"Take assshhlong as you neeeed, doveling," I mumbled, rolling onto my back on the floor. The room was spinning. "Fuck. I need a minute too. Aoife-aoife-aoife...iiiish there anything to make...her blood...less...bubbly?" I giggled as I struggled to think of the right words. I pushed the heels of my hands against my closed eyes. "Or else I don't know how I'm going to do this..."

"Awe, no, don't do that. Drunk Felkyn might be amusing enough to get me through this," Danielle said with a thin reedy laugh. She sat up but swayed. How many more times did we have to do this?

"Unfortunately, this doesn't happen often enough for us to know how to remedy it," Declan explained, coming over and helping me sit up. The room still pulsed, but at least it wasn't spinning.

Aoife approached Danielle with a mug of something for the pain, but Danielle waved it away.

"I'm okay," she insisted, but she rubbed the spot on her neck where I'd slashed. "But we might need to tie me down."

I crawled back up onto the bed. "And I'll drink from different spots, to—"

"Vary the pain?" she joked, running a hand up my arm.

While Declan went to find things to bind her limbs to the bed, I lined myself up over her, placing my knee between her thighs and pressing her pelvis into the bed with my hip. Still a little blood-drunk, I waffled on where to bite next. I almost dove back into her neck but changed my mind and grabbed fistfuls of her shirt and tore it open over her left breast.

She gasped and started to protest, but I forced her shoulders back into the bed.

"Grab the pillows or the headboard, or something," I murmured, my lips hovering above the artery in her upper pectoral. "And remember not to scream or Aoife will kill you."

CHAPTER 24

DANIELLE

My arteries were on fire. I drew in a lungful of air to help steady me through the pain, but it only sent a burning through my chest. The blood being pulled from my body deprived my organs of the oxygen they needed, making everything burn—especially my lungs.

They'd bound my legs by the ankles to the footboard, but my wrists had writhed free of their restraints. I threw my arms behind my head and dug my nails into the underside of the pillow behind me. I tried to keep my mouth clamped shut as a violent shudder ripped through my limbs, and I almost succeeded at staying silent, but three more seconds of the pain was too much.

The scream was barely out of my half-filled lungs when the searing pain receded. I locked my jaw and silence filled the room, but only for a moment. A second, terrified cry filled the air, this one from Libby down the hall. I'd woken her. Declan swore and his pounding footsteps retreated from the room.

"I'm sorry," I mumbled. I opened my eyes and through my swimming vision caught sight of Declan's back before he disappeared into the hall. I'd promised I wouldn't scream. It had always taken a lot to get me to scream, but I had no idea this would be anywhere near that threshold.

"I'm sorry, dove. I'm so sorry," Felkyn murmured, lifting his head from the tear he'd made in my sweats so he could access the artery in my inner thigh. I wanted to make a joke about the absurdly intimate place he'd chosen to bite this time, but the sight of my blood smeared across his mouth and chin curdled the humor on my tongue. Normally feeding wasn't as messy, but my pained writhing had made it harder for him to contain the flow of blood into his mouth.

"I woke Libby when I said I wouldn't." My voice had no strength behind it and came out as more of a whine than anything.

"We'll find it in us to forgive you if you let me give you something to knock you out for this part," Aoife said, appearing by my shoulder, already holding the draught she was threatening me with.

"No," I said, trying to lift my hand to rub my face, but my muscles were too oxygen deprived. Instead, I closed my eyes tight to try to steady my vision. When I opened them again, I could see straight, but through a long, dark tunnel.

He didn't need to tell me we were close. My heart was racing to circulate my thinned blood, and my lungs labored to pull in as much air as possible to fuel my organs. And I was so cold, it took everything left in my jaw muscles to keep my teeth from chattering.

"I'm sorry," he said again, slurring drunkenly. He put his hand to my cheek, and I wasn't sure if it was his hand or my jaw that was trembling. "It isn't supposed to be like this. It's your last moments alive and you have to spend it in such agony."

"I'm right as rain, sunshine," I told him through my chattering teeth. "I've had periods worse than this."

My weak humor didn't lessen the guilt in his eyes. He knew what it meant when I resorted to snark: I was afraid. Afraid, but not backing down.

We were too far now to back out, even if I wanted to. We were closer to the other side now, so we needed to keep going. The pain I could deal with, but the cold was another story.

He helped my limp torso into a sitting position and climbed onto the bed behind me, laying me back against his chest. His warm arms wrapped around me, but I barely felt the relief. He brushed my hair away from my neck and ran his knuckles down my jaw, coaxing my head back and to the side against his shoulder.

"This will be it, this time," he murmured softly, his lips at my ear. Again, it would be intimate if I wasn't nearly drained and imagining how blue I must look. "Still want this?"

I barely heard him over the rushing sound in my ears. I wasn't sure if it was a panic attack brewing or just the blood rushing to deliver oxygen to my brain. I tried to ignore it, working my tongue around my suddenly dry mouth. I was too weak to speak, but I put some of the last of my strength into a single nod.

I jerked involuntarily when his warm lips met the shivering skin of my neck. His fangs ripped at my flesh, and again I was encased in pain.

As the pain rose to what I imagined—or hoped—was the final crescendo, my mouth opened to scream again. But he pressed his arm against my mouth, not to stifle my scream, but to put his wrist between my jaw before it clenched. The suddenness startled me into silence, but the pain hadn't lessened.

Now, love. His voice rang in my head. Though I was in pain still, I almost sighed at hearing his voice in my head again. I had to be close to death for my mental block to give way to him. *Bite!*

The pain built and sharpened, and my jaw clenched automatically against another scream, hard enough for my teeth to tear into his wrist. In the horrifying moment that I felt my heart stop, warm blood poured from his wrist into my mouth.

"Hey, hit the lights before she comes to," a soft, airy voice spoke near my ear, but he wasn't talking to me. A hand brushed through my hair soothingly.

I hadn't even realized that light was assaulting my closed eyelids until the flipping of a switch echoed in the silent room. Calling the room silent, though, was inaccurate because it was anything but. Electricity buzzed in the walls, even after the lights shut off. The air conditioning roared across the house and whistled in the ducts. Water thundered in the pipes from a previously flushed toilet and splashed in a bathroom sink. I could hear Declan clearly through multiple walls as he softly spoke to Libby about going back to bed.

But at least the lights were turned low. Yet as my eyelids fluttered, details of the room peeked through clear as day. The abundant fragrance from dozens of herbs hit my nose with an intensity so great I nearly gagged. I groaned and rolled my head to the side, pressing my eyes closed tight in disgust.

"If the smells bother you, you don't have to breathe them in. It'll be instinctual for a while, but you no longer need to breathe," the low, gentle voice murmured into my ear, soft enough that it didn't aggravate my heightened hearing.

Felkyn. I realized I was still in his arms as he gently brushed hair off my face and kissed my forehead.

I'd drowned before and been resuscitated, and reintroducing air to my lungs had been traumatic, but waking and not needing air was something my brain couldn't comprehend. My processes shorted out, and panic spiked. Only this time it didn't bring the blood pounding in my ears because I had no pulse anymore.

"Easy," Felkyn said softly, above me. He gripped my shoulders and eased himself out from under me. He lowered me down onto my back. "I'm sorry, that was a stupid way to handle it. It's okay. Here..." He lay on his side beside me and pulled me into his arms, guiding my face to his chest. "Breathe all you want. Don't try to fight instinct yet. Don't worry. Just breathe me in and focus on me, nothing else. It's okay."

Eyes still closed, I curled into him, and he pressed his hands over my ears, muffling the background noise that was so loud. Blocking the sound helped me focus on inhaling his scent without being overstimulated. He smelled of our laundry detergent and of soap. There were other scents to him as well that were usually so subtle I grouped them all together, but now they stood out separately. There was the salty smell of ocean spray and hot sand as well as bow rosin and antique wood stain from the instruments in his studio.

Slowly, my panic receded, and I uncurled from the fetal position. He eased his hands off my ears, and sound returned, but it wasn't overwhelming like before. Already, I was adjusting to my heightened senses.

All pain was gone. The aches and pains from fighting against restraints and being temporarily oxygen deprived were gone. My nasal cavity and throat, which had burned ever since I was resuscitated, felt normal. My neck, which had been tender with bruises, felt fine to the touch.

Carefully, I opened my eyes. It was dark in the room—I knew this—yet it only seemed dim. I could make out all the details of Felkyn's beautiful face as it broke into a dazzling smile.

There's my beautiful phoenix, he said, but his mouth didn't move. Telepathy. He could communicate silently with me again!

Is this thing on? I sent to him. I was winging it, merely guessing it was like when I reached into his mind as a mortal witch.

"Like a pro, already," he said aloud, grinning. He cupped my face with both hands and leaned in to kiss me.

"Can we turn the lights on now?" Aoife cut in before Felkyn's lips met mine.

"Yeah, rip off the band-aid," I told her, leaning back.

The lights weren't as harsh as I expected. But it was garish and everything seemed hyper-detailed. My eyes hadn't been exactly twenty-twenty before, but now they were that and more.

"It's really not fair," Aoife said, frowning as she inspected me from the other side of the queen bed. "How you can go from pale, shivering, and blue to femme fatale in, like, five minutes!"

When I frowned in confusion, my skin felt tight around my lips. I rubbed my mouth and jaw, and my hand came away red with partly congealed blood. I looked down at myself and realized I was covered in blood from my neck to the torn hole in my shirt, and one leg of my sweatpants was sticky with it as well. *Holy shit.* I groaned and pulled at the ends of my hair, which were crusty with blood as well.

"Definitely don't look at your reflection until after you've showered," she said quickly as I started to turn toward the mirror. "I mean, you're gorgeous. But you also look like a Final Girl..."

F elkyn was waiting with a towel when I shut the water off. He wrapped it around my shoulders and grabbed another for my hair, but I laughed him off.

"You don't have to pamper me." I chuckled, taking the towel from him. "I'm a strong Lapsus now, remember? I can dry my own hair."

"I know that." He grinned and booped my nose with a corner of the towel. He leaned forward and kissed my lips. "I can't help wanting to pamper you, though, my phoenix."

"You need to retire phoenix as a pet name," I said, tucking my hair behind my ear. "It doesn't apply anymore."

"You never know," he said, smirking furtively, slipping his arms inside the folds of the towel around my shoulders and pulling my hips against his. "You've always been anomalous. Maybe you'll defy the rules here too."

"Hmm, doubtful. I'm full Lapsi now. Goodbye magic," I chided him, stepping back from him. "Give me a few minutes to dry off and get dressed, then take me to dinner?"

"Heh, sure thing, dove." He chuckled and rolled his eyes. "I shifted home and grabbed you some clothes. I'll see you in a few."

Minutes later, dry and dressed, I finally looked at myself in the mirror. The same large brown eyes greeted me. My straight brown hair would forever be just past my collarbones. The pale scar in my eyebrow had never healed, and now it never would.

All in all, I looked ninety percent the same as I had that morning, yet somehow I looked the best I ever had without makeup. Aside from the scars which hadn't disappeared with the change, my skin was flawless and a healthy pink in all the right places. And I would always look like this, as long as I was fed.

Frowning, I looked down at my wrists and the brands that were still visible. The brands that'd nearly bound me to servitude. But I'd thwarted that plan, and now they could never use me again. As soon as they figured out I was Lapsi, they'd leave me alone forever. Even if I'd always been anomalous, I wasn't in this.

To test it, I picked up a scented candle Aoife kept on the bathroom vanity. *It won't work,* I told myself, staring at the blackened wick. *Please don't work.*

I concentrated on it like I'd always done before. Willing it to light.

With a small hiss, a lick of flame ignited the wick, wavering in the breeze from the bathroom exhaust fan.

Fuck.

AMELIA ROSE

The End

ACKNOWLEDGMENTS

Hello again, dearest reader! You will always be the first that I thank at the end of my books. Without you, this whole thing is pointless and unfulfilling. I do all of this for those that take the chance on me, and that make it through these pages of my weird brain. I love you, and thank you from the bottom of my heart.

Next, as always, by awesome ride or die beta reader, Lisa. You are a rockstar, and I loved your commentary on this one!

I listened to a lot a lot a lot of Voilà, Chrissy Costanza, Black Veil Brides, and Andy Black while writing, editing, and illustrating this book. I can feel their presence kissing these pages, even if readers can't. Thank you, you wonderful musicians for vibing with my book and directing my fingers to the keys, my pen to my tablet, and my eyes through the lines.

And thank you to everyone in my life that supports and bears with me through the crazy times of writing, editing, and designing. I become hyper-fixated and sleep deprived, and just a little bit mad. Thank you for those that see this, and that give me the proper space, or make me eat or sleep.

I love you all, thank you, thank you, thank you!

Please Review

Please tell me and others what you thought of this book? Thank you so much for reading my story. Your eyes on the page mean the world to me. If you feel comfortable doing so, I implore you to leave a rating and review for this book on any of the e-commerce or booky platforms. Reviews (whether good, bad, or neutral) are invaluable to authors. They help us see where we need to improve, and help us get our books into more hands.

Don't miss out!

Visit the website below and you can sign up to receive emails whenever Amelia Rose publishes a new book. There's no charge and no obligation.

https://books2read.com/r/B-A-LGDZ-NHULG

BOOKS 2 READ

Connecting independent readers to independent writers.

About the Author

Amelia Rose has a BA in English and Classical Humanities, but barely remembers any Latin. She lives in Ohio with her husband, and fills every moment of her free time with writing, drawing, making beaded jewelry, or constructing cardboard sculptures. She loves dancing shamelessly to all kinds of music, obsessing over musicals, devouring horror movies—the gorier the better—and going to concerts. She never passes up the chance to ride a rollercoaster or get kisses from a dog.